PRAISE FOR SEAN CHERCOVER

THE DEVIL'S GAME

"A rocket of a conspiracy thriller, *The Devil's Game* blasts the reader from Liberia to Norway to the heart of the USA, taking no prisoners along the way. Daniel Byrne is a hero's hero; I can't wait to see more of Byrne—and (as always) more Chercover."

—Gregg Hurwitz, *New York Times* bestselling author of
Don't Look Back

"Snappy, smart, and satisfying, it makes for a compulsive read."
—Chelsea Cain, *New York Times* bestselling author of *One Kick*

"An exceptional read. Explosive and gripping, this is everything you want in a thriller, and some of the smoothest writing you'll ever hope to read."

—Blake Crouch, bestselling author of *Dark Matter* and the
Wayward Pines trilogy

"Listen to me. Read Sean Chercover."
—Robert Crais, #1 *New York Times* bestselling author of *Taken*

"Breathtaking. Science and technology meet morality head-on in this fast-paced thriller."

—*Booklist*

"*The Trinity Game* is a rare find. Heart-pounding cinematic action, unpredictable twists, and wonderful characters—all packed into a fascinating story. What a thrilling ride! I loved it from the start, couldn't put it down, and was sorry to see it end. You have got to read this book!"

—Marcia Clark, *New York Times* bestselling author of *Blood Defense*

"*The Trinity Game* swept me up from page one. High-octane and thought provoking—a powerful combination."

—Meg Gardiner, Edgar Award–winning author of *Ransom River*

"*The Da Vinci Code* meets *The Dead Zone* in Sean Chercover's *The Trinity Game*, a fascinating thriller that catapults us headlong into Vatican intrigue, global conspiracies, complex family relationships, and nonstop excitement."

—Joseph Finder, *New York Times* bestselling author of *Paranoia* and *Buried Secrets*

"This is no ordinary thriller. Chercover challenges his readers to get their heads around some big ideas. Powerful and moving."

—*Booklist*

THE
SAVIOR'S
GAME

OTHER TITLES BY SEAN CHERCOVER

THE
SAVIOR'S
GAME

SEAN CHERCOVER

THOMAS & MERCER

Text copyright ©2017 by Sean Chercover

Published by Thomas & Mercer, Seattle

www.apub.com

Amazon, the Amazon logo, and Thomas & Mercer are trademarks of Amazon.com, Inc., or its affiliates.

ISBN-13: 9781477848791 (hardcover)
ISBN-10: 1477848797 (hardcover)
ISBN-13: 9781503944602 (paperback)
ISBN-10: 1503944603 (paperback)

Cover design by Christian Fuenfhausen

Printed in the United States of America

First edition

For Firedog

1
=

I t was the same room.

The same room, bathed in the same not-quite-orange glow that presages sunset. Daniel Byrne let out the breath he was holding and filled his lungs again. He crossed the antique living room rug, toward the tiled entrance hall. At the end of the hallway, a solid wooden door, painted British racing green.

Daniel had never passed through that door, in either direction, but he knew this apartment. He knew the bedroom in back was painted red, the same shade as his boyhood bedroom at 2601 General Pershing Street, in uptown New Orleans. He knew there was a 1920s armoire—aromatic Spanish cedar, natural finish, white porcelain knobs—in the bedroom. It had been in Tim Trinity's room of that same childhood home. Before seeing it here three months ago, Daniel hadn't laid eyes on it since he was thirteen.

Weirder still, the handwoven rug he now crossed had been in the living room of Kara Singh's London flat. The rug had burned to ash when Conrad Winter's men torched her building down to the foundation.

And yet, here it lay, the wool soft under Daniel's bare feet. Restored.

He walked to the French doors, knowing exactly what he would see when he opened them and stepped onto the balcony: teak furniture with green-and-white-striped cushions, same as the other four times. And beyond the balcony wall, the same almost-tropical seaside town. Coconut palms in abundance, and a subtly fragrant breeze that said West Indies, but the low-rise buildings looked more Southern California—a lot of white stucco and Spanish terra-cotta roofs, with a sprinkling of art deco here and there. Cars parked on the street below ran the gamut from beater to Benz. So, a reasonably prosperous seaside town, bathed in the hyper-realistic glow of what filmmakers call *magic hour*.

It seemed Daniel was the only person in this town. At least, he couldn't see anyone else from this balcony. Last time, he'd stood here for maybe fifteen minutes before trying, once more, to leave the apartment.

Only a fool would expect a different result the fifth time. He glanced again at the green door as he moved back inside to the kitchen. *Front door is not the way out of here.*

He grabbed a bottle of water from the well-stocked fridge and returned to the balcony. He nursed the water until the bottle was empty, watching the whole time. A quick trip inside for a new bottle of water, then back to the balcony, watching.

When the water was gone, he judged he'd been on the balcony the better part of an hour. He'd seen not a soul, not even an airplane in the sky, and he'd heard no voices or car engines or distant noises. Just the sound of the breeze, and the rhythmic beat of the surf hitting the shore, perhaps two or three blocks to the west.

But strangest of all was the sun. The sun had stayed exactly where it was in the sky, not a millimeter lower since he'd arrived. And yet, the sound of the surf told Daniel the ocean was moving at a normal pace. And since tides were caused by the gravitational pull of the moon, the moon must be moving at a normal pace, relative to the Earth.

Which didn't easily jibe with the Earth not rotating, freezing the sun's position in the sky.

It would take some getting used to.

Remembering shoes he'd seen in the bedroom before, Daniel stepped inside, leaving the balcony doors standing wide.

The bedroom was as expected—red walls, cedar armoire, a pair of brown leather shoes beside the bed. Daniel sat on the bed and picked them up, turning them over in his hands. Crepe rubber soles, waxed leather uppers with a thick seam sewn up the middle. More foot shaped than shoe shaped, they were completely broken in, contours suggesting many miles, wet and dry, on their owner's feet.

He slipped his bare feet into the shoes. Perfect fit. These were clearly his shoes and no one else's, but he could not recall having worn them before.

He laced up the shoes, walked back through the living room, stepped out onto the balcony, and approached the white half wall. The wall came up to just below his rib cage and boasted dozens of round terra-cotta-lined holes, which served to let some natural light pass through.

He felt the rough texture of the stucco surface on his hands, leaned forward over the wall, and looked down past another balcony. A patio with a metal loveseat and a couple of young coconut palms in large terra-cotta planters lay directly below, two stories down.

Probably wouldn't kill him, but far enough for a broken ankle or two.

He hoisted himself up and swung his legs over so that he was sitting on the wall, his feet dangling. He raised his gaze, fixed his eyes on the windows of the building directly across the street, and after a few slow, centering breaths, turned to face the balcony, using the lowest terra-cotta holes as toeholds.

There hadn't been a sound from anywhere within or near the building, but if there were occupants below, they might not assume a strange man swinging onto their balcony from above was a friendly visitor.

"If there's anybody below," Daniel called out, "my front door is not working—it's stuck—so I'm gonna climb down the balconies. I'm peaceful and unarmed."

He felt foolish talking to no one—and he felt quite certain that there was no one—but better to play it safe. He'd appreciate the same courtesy.

Do unto others, as the man said.

"Awright, coming down now."

Daniel squatted against the outside of the half wall, shifting his hands into the holes, keeping his center of gravity as close to the building as possible. He pulled his feet out of their toeholds, tensing his core and back, and slowly let gravity take his legs. He shifted his right hand lower, then his left, and then swung his legs away from the wall, added to their momentum as they pendulumed back, and released his grip.

He cleared the balcony wall below by more than he needed to, landing on his feet with too much forward momentum, but managed to lurch-step his way to a stop just short of tumbling over the furniture. The French doors were closed, the shutters behind them shut.

No evidence of neighbors.

Daniel repeated the process on this level, calling down to no one before lowering himself and dropping to the patio below.

Time to find out where the hell he was.

2

The street itself looked normal and well maintained.

So where *was* everyone?

Daniel stopped walking and stood on the yellow line in the middle of the road. He was forgetting something important. He concentrated for a moment but could not recall what it was. He looked at the cars parked along both curbs. Something about them felt . . . he didn't know what, exactly, but there was definitely something wrong about them.

He scanned both sides of the street. The cars themselves were just fine, but the assortment—this particular assortment—felt somehow *curated*, as though he were walking through a Hollywood film set. At the same time, this moment felt more real than any previous moment of his life.

Then he remembered what he was forgetting. The idea he'd had up on the balcony.

Get to the ground, read the license plates, and you'll know where you are.

Why had his mind resisted remembering that idea? And why did it now resist looking?

In Daniel's peripheral vision, the license plates appeared perfectly normal, but even *intending* to focus on a single plate triggered intense unease, physically and emotionally. Queasiness in the pit of the gut, akin to the physical symptoms of both guilt and dread.

Just look at it.

He forced his attention onto a single plate, the one on the black Tesla to his right. The plate blurred as he looked, and then became increasingly bright, until it glowed—no longer just reflecting but emitting a brilliant white light of its own.

Daniel had to look away when it started to feel like staring at the sun. He dropped his gaze to the pavement, blinking water from his eyes, watching the ghost image of a rectangular sun explode anew with each blink, until it slowly faded and no longer threatened to trigger a full-blown headache.

Message received: The license plates do not wish to be examined.

Daniel walked on. The buildings on either side of the street looked like apartments, or condos. Nice, but without ostentation. He spotted a newspaper box at the corner and jogged over to it. The paper's front page was pressed against the inside of the clear plastic window, but when he looked at it, the print blurred out of focus and the paper began to glow white.

Again he had to look away, eyes watering, head throbbing, gut knotted with guilt, or dread, or maybe both. He returned his gaze to the ground, braced his hands on his knees, and stayed that way until the symptoms subsided.

Once confident he wouldn't pass out, he straightened, took a couple of deep breaths, and made a token effort to read the name on the street sign above. As soon as the sign began to blur, he averted his eyes.

Not productive. This town will hurt you if you try to identify it.

He focused on the solidity of the pavement underfoot, the warmth of the sunlight on his face. He turned left—west—onto the street that was shy about its name. Looking ahead, he could see that the street ran downhill for five blocks, ending in a T intersection. Beyond the intersection there was a wide sandy beach, and then the sea, glittering like a field of broken glass beneath the nuclear furnace in the sky. He held a hand up to shade his eyes.

The surf sounded unnaturally close—he'd guessed two or maybe three blocks if the blocks were short. The sound conflicted with the five blocks his eyes now registered, and the resulting cognitive dissonance was unnerving.

Despite the initial discomfort, the discrepancy was explainable after a moment's thought. With no people or machines moving about to deflect sound waves or create competing noise, the surf would indeed sound louder than expected.

But try as he might, Daniel still couldn't explain the sky.

Proposition One: The sun doesn't move in the sky, so the Earth is barely rotating, if at all.

Proposition Two: Gravity and tides and atmosphere are all normal, so the Earth is rotating at normal speed.

Both propositions could not be true.

And yet.

He kept walking, toward the immobile sun. In the second block, apartment buildings gave way to detached one- and two-story houses. Facing into the sun wasn't helping Daniel's headache, so he turned right, the sun now to his left, and walked down an alley, flanked on both sides by wooden backyard fences and gates, upper-floor windows reflecting the sky.

Nobody home.

And yet: At the foot of one backyard gate, five beer bottles lay scattered. Stubby brown bottles. Red Stripe lager. Somebody'd drank that beer and left those bottles.

He turned right again at the end of the alley, putting the sun behind him. His shadow stretched forward from his feet along the road, leading the way uphill.

Aside from the slope to the beach, it was a flat town, almost universally low-rise, the tallest buildings perhaps six stories. But as Daniel turned the corner, the one exception revealed itself, and he heard himself gasp as he came to a stop, staring.

The single white tower rose in the distance to an impossible height. He guessed the building was about six miles to the east, but if that were true, it would have to be at least three hundred stories tall.

He set off at a brisk pace, uphill to where the road leveled and then through town, block after block of mostly two-story homes with alleys running between backyard fences. As the high-rise got closer, he estimated it was easily twice the height of the tallest building on Earth.

Wait.

Daniel made himself a statue. Yes, the rumble of a car nearby. The engine noise died. Then a car door closing. And now footsteps— leather soles on the pavement ahead.

He set off at a jog, following the sound around the next corner, where he saw a man striding along the sidewalk in his direction, maybe thirty paces away.

Late twenties, athletic build, wearing a mustard-yellow linen suit and white leather cowboy boots. The man wore his hair slicked back, his face clean shaven. He tossed Daniel a pleasant smile, as you do to a passing stranger, but did not slow as he approached.

Daniel raised a hand. "Excuse me. Do you—" He gestured at the empty street. "This may sound odd, but where is everybody?"

The man stopped walking. His smile broadened. He said, "Hello, Daniel," as he slid his right hand into his jacket, reaching under his left armpit.

Gun.

Daniel bolted across the street and dived beside a parked sedan, pistol fire barking from behind, rounds pinging off concrete and thunking into sheet metal, the car's side windows exploding above his head. He scrambled to get his feet under him, then ran in a half crouch, blocking the sides of his head with his forearms, stealing a glance to locate the gunman—

—now crossing the street. Not running, but moving with a relaxed stride.

"Daniel," the man called out. "Stop. You're only gonna die tired."

There was another alley ahead on the right—*get around the corner, find cover, find a weapon*—but it was still ten yards to the corner. All the other man had to do was jog a few yards and he'd have Daniel in his sights. An easy kill. But the man maintained a leisurely pace as Daniel sprinted away.

"Seriously, man. Noah says you gotta go. Don't make me break a sweat."

Seven yards to the corner.

"Trust me, you don't even want to be here, not really."

Four yards.

"Just stop running, and—"

Three.

"—I'll make it quick and you won't ever have to come back."

Daniel flung his right arm out, slapping the wall of the building, swinging himself around the corner near full speed, skidding to a stop.

Shit. Nothing to hide behind, not even a recycling bin. He lunged three steps to his right and yanked on the handle of a backyard gate.

Locked.

He sprinted down the alley, jerking the handles of a few more locked gates as he passed. A thunderous crash of metal from behind, and he spun to see—

—two large dumpsters, now blocking the way back, lying on their sides like they'd toppled in from either side of the alley.

There had been no dumpsters anywhere when Daniel had entered the alley.

Another metallic crash from behind and he spun forward. A roll-down iron gate, like the kind that protects storefronts in New York City at night, now spanned the distance between buildings, blocking the other end of the alley completely.

He was trapped.

Cowboy boots scuffed along the sidewalk behind the overturned dumpsters.

Something moved to his right. The wooden backyard gate across the alley creaked open. A woman in her forties stood just inside the gate. She wore blue jeans and a black T-shirt that said *Wake Up!* in white brushstroke. Glasses with purple frames. Wild hair. She invited Daniel forward with an impatient nod of her chin.

Daniel dashed through the open gate and the woman closed it behind him. Up close, her hair wasn't quite as anarchic as it first appeared. She clearly cultivated the rebel look, making a statement while keeping it from going full-tilt dreadlock.

"Daniel." Her accent pegged her from the Boston area, and although Daniel had never seen this woman before, he knew her voice. It was the voice that had taken up residence in his head a few months earlier, when he was struck with the condition known—to those who knew most about it—as Anomalous Information Transfer, or AIT.

The last three months had bordered on insanity for Daniel. Intense dreams of being hit by lightning, strange visions that hit like fits beyond his control, and a disembodied voice popping into his head at random intervals, speaking cryptic warnings that only he could hear. A psychologically bumpy ride, even before a man in a yellow suit started shooting at him and large metal objects started crashing into existence out of thin air.

The gunman's footfalls echoed closer, now past the dumpsters, scraping on the pavement inside the alley.

The woman pushed the glasses up her nose and peered down through the twin half moons of her bifocal lenses. She placed her palm flat against Daniel's chest. After a moment, she said, "Noah's soldiers are all around. We've got to get you out of here."

Daniel said, "I don't know you, but I know your voice. And I don't know anyone named Noah, but the man out there is trying to kill me, so I'm all for getting me out of here."

She nodded once, pulled her hand back, and poked Daniel's forehead with her index finger.

The world began spinning. Not like on a carnival midway ride—more like at the flat-on-your-back ending of an alcohol-soaked all-nighter.

"Let go, Daniel. Just relax and let go." With each word, her voice receded farther into the distance, until it was just a whisper on the wind. "Go home."

Daniel's vision dimmed and he could feel his consciousness slipping, descending through his body, his legs, flowing through the soles of his feet and into the ground below.

Into darkness. And silence.

3

Bathsheba, Barbados

Daniel opened his eyes. He was sitting seiza—kneeling on the floor, hands cupped loosely in his lap, zafu cushion supporting his butt. He blinked as his eyes adjusted. A single candle flickered on the floor, four feet in front of him. Beyond the reach of the candlelight, the room was washed in moonlight, which spilled in through the open slats of the shuttered window to his right.

Sounds also spilled in through the window—the high-pitched *bleep-bleep, bleep-bleep* of tree frogs all around, and the gentle rhythm of the surf kissing the beach at the bottom of the hill.

The taste of cinnamon on his tongue began to ease, and he remembered where he was.

His living room. His rental cottage. Barbados.

Meditating.

Daniel felt a smile invade his face. He'd done it. He'd entered the vision *on purpose.*

Being there on purpose had changed things. The previous four times, the vision of the apartment in the seaside town had come as spontaneous attacks of AIT. And each time, the vision had ended when he'd tried to leave the apartment by the front door. This time, entering the vision from meditation, he'd had the presence of mind to figure another way out. He'd had more control this time, felt deeper inside the vision, experiencing it rather than watching it unfold. It hadn't been some dream version of Daniel climbing down balconies and choosing which way to turn along streets and alleys, talking to the gunman, running for his life. It had been his conscious self.

A huge step. Proof that AIT was susceptible to influence. A milestone. But whatever the hell the visions and voices were actually trying to *say* . . . he still hadn't a clue.

A man in a yellow suit had tried to kill Daniel on behalf of someone named Noah, and a woman—with the same voice as the voice in Daniel's head—had saved him. In a town where you can't leave your apartment by the front door and the sun never moves in the sky and certain things glow so brightly you can't look at them.

Not much crazier than your average dream while sleeping, but this was not a dream. It was an AIT vision, and it was supposed to mean something. Daniel had absolutely no idea what.

He stood and stretched, put the candle on his roll-top desk. Walked to the kitchen, opened the fridge, and stuck his face into the cold light. Stood there for a minute, plucking his shirtfront away from his chest, letting a little cool air in.

He grabbed a bottle of 10 Saints from the fridge, pried the cap off using the wall-mounted bottle opener above the recycling bin. A couple deep swigs of beer washed the remaining cinnamon taste from his mouth. He took the rest of the bottle back to the desk in the living room and switched on the lamp as he sat.

Kara Singh had lived with voices in her head for six years, and she'd kept journals—transcriptions of the voices and detailed descriptions of her visions. The information she'd recorded hadn't revealed the cause of her affliction, but it had been key to uncovering a brutal conspiracy—one Daniel could only partially subvert, and at the cost of many lives.

Kara's journals had either burned or been stolen by the men Conrad Winter sent to torch her building, and the voices AIT inflicted upon her for six years had simply vanished, with no more explanation than why they'd come in the first place.

Whatever the cause of this strange condition, most of the world knew it as the Trinity Phenomenon—after Daniel's uncle, the late Reverend Tim Trinity, television evangelist and grifter extraordinaire. Trinity's voices and visions had predicted the future. Kara's had been more opaque but wider ranging, also revealing events of the past. Daniel had also met a plague-infected soldier with the condition, who believed himself possessed by Satan. There were over ten thousand confirmed cases by now, and certainly more than ten times as many unconfirmed. But until two weeks ago, Tim Trinity's was the only case known to the public.

Two weeks ago, Julia Rothman's *The Truth (So Far) about Trinity* had been published, and published huge. Number one on every list around the world, dissected and debated breathlessly on cable news channels, dominating social media, *breaking the Internet*. Even here in Barbados, where tourists came to escape the reality of their lives, the book was everywhere. Towering displays in the book department of every Cave Shepherd, every resort gift shop, every newsagent's store.

At taxi stands and in supermarket checkout lines, in restaurants and churches and doctors' waiting rooms, burning from the screens of Kindles under beach umbrellas . . . Bajans and tourists alike—*everyone* was reading it, talking about it, reporting on it, and debating it. It was the universal topic of conversation around the globe. There was no avoiding it.

The whole world was having a bumpy ride, adjusting to the reality shift.

Julia's investigation revealed six cases of Anomalous Information Transfer. Three cases were only mentioned in brief summary, with no identifying information. In one, the sufferer had been committed to a mental hospital, and the other two were not willing to come forward publicly.

But the other three—an encyclopedia salesman in New Orleans, a farm wife in Germany, and an unemployed bicycle mechanic in Tokyo—wanted their stories told. They were all under great stress because of their condition, but in Julia's estimation they were not insane. They all heard voices. All had conscious dreams they called visions. All kept records of what they dreamed and what the voices told them.

And for each of these three individuals, in at least two verifiable instances, the voices and visions had provided information the sufferers could not possibly have known.

Somehow, these people had predicted the future.

That their predictions were mundane was beside the point. Tim Trinity's predictions had also been mundane, until they weren't. Until they threw the entire nation into a panic.

Julia's book contained no mention of a Dr. Kara Singh, or any details of her case. She had honored Kara's request to be left out of it completely.

Julia had found these people by her own investigation, but Daniel had, with the approval of his former boss, given her some other leads. Doctors who studied the phenomenon, allies of the Fleur-de-Lis Foundation who could be trusted to reveal only as much as the Foundation's managing director, Carter Ames, was willing to reveal at the time.

Thus Ames had shaped the public story by proxy, and the world learned that there existed "probably a few thousand" cases of AIT worldwide, which underestimated the truth by at least a hundred thousand. The doctors had been sure to emphasize how miniscule a few thousand was, on a planet of seven billion people, and they'd given no indication that it was spreading.

But it was spreading, and the rate of spread was accelerating. You couldn't call it a contagion in the traditional sense, but it was acting like one.

Carter's puppets were also successful in coining the moniker Anomalous Information Transfer, which seemed like an appropriately scientific, evidence-based name. But such was the mystique of Tim Trinity, that most people still called it the Trinity Phenomenon, even after reading Julia's book.

Whatever you called it, whatever it was, it was spreading fast. And Daniel had it.

AIT had come on strong with him, ramping up over the course of just a week. Intense nightmares about being hit by lightning, a woman's voice—the voice that belonged to the woman in his most recent vision—imploring him to pay attention and telling of some unspecified past or future disaster that had left (or would leave) over a thousand dead. And now, for the fifth time, he'd had the hyper-realistic vision of that apartment in the seaside town with the frozen sun.

Daniel pulled a notebook from the top drawer of his desk. His own handwriting on the cover:

A/T Journal #3

He flipped about a third of the way into the notebook, to the first blank page, and plucked a pencil from the earthenware coffee mug on the desk. He took his mind back to the beginning of the meditation session—

Wait.

The sound of a car pulling slowly up the road outside. But no headlights swept the windows as it turned onto Daniel's street.

The driver was running dark.

The engine noise died, maybe four houses away. Someone opened and shut the door, making as little sound as possible. Daniel shot a glance at his watch. Two thirty-five.

Not infrequently, one of the English surfer dudes next door stayed out past closing time. Could be he was trying to get home without waking the street. But the surfer dudes drove an ancient Suzuki jeep with a muffler that rattled. This machine was smooth running and rattle-free.

Daniel switched off the lamp and blew out the candle. He crept to the open slats of the shuttered window and peeked through. Although there were no streetlights on this block, the moon was high and the sky cloudless. He could see the man well enough, but for a second he just didn't believe it.

White cowboy boots, yellow linen suit, hair slicked back. The suit had been tailored to minimize the gun's bulge under the left armpit, but thanks to the vision, Daniel knew to look for it.

The man was now three houses away, walking a straight line toward this house, a white panel van parked on the road behind him.

Daniel dashed from the window, snatched a backpack from the closet, and tore through the desk—cash, wallet, passports, cell phone, extra SIM card, journals, locker key, and his uncle's old switchblade. He ran to the back bedroom and closed the door behind him. He switched on the bedside lamp and slipped into a pair of shoes.

The bedroom window's sash was already up—Daniel had left it wide to draw a cross breeze. Now he deployed the switchblade and cut along the bottom and both sides of the screen, making a giant flap.

He paused, heard his front door's dead bolt click open. Then the man's cowboy boots, leather soles scuffing quietly into the living room.

Daniel tossed the backpack through the screen flap, followed it, and turned to pull the window down to the sill. With the darkness outside and the bedside lamp on, the glass would act to mirror the inside of the room.

He crept through the tiny, unfenced yard, hitching the pack onto his back, then dashed across the street, ducking behind a rusty Daihatsu hatchback, and ran—staying low and keeping to the shadows—four houses down, then cut through a backyard and stopped between two houses, the white panel van parked ahead on his left.

The van's cockpit was empty, but the cargo section was windowless. No way to know if there was someone in back. Daniel crept forward, switchblade in hand, inching closer to the rear doors. He stopped and listened hard.

No sound from inside.

He reached for the handle with his left hand while raising the blade in his right, thinking: *Good chance this gets ugly fast . . .*

He took a breath, opened the door, and breathed out.

No one inside.

Instead, there was a gurney bolted to the floor, thick leather restraints hanging from its chrome rails. Some kind of medical machine next to the gurney, and an IV stand.

Daniel used his phone's little flashlight to get a better look, and felt his groin turn to ice.

It was an ECT machine.

Electroconvulsive therapy.

Shock treatments.

A polite term for scrambling your brain's electrical wiring.

Daniel spun on his heel and took off running.

4

Greenwich Village, New York City

The afternoon sun hung just above the rooftops and the temperature stood at freezing and the trees were naked. Although there was no snow on the ground, thousands of fat flakes eddied above the pavement, like hovercraft bumper cars. They would settle in for the night, but tomorrow's sun would melt them and late November's dry air would suck them up and it would be as if they'd never existed.

Daniel reckoned he had a long, cold night ahead. After only a few hours in New York, he could already feel his tanned face drying out, getting ready to peel. He handed some cash to the cab driver and stepped out onto the sidewalk. He closed the zipper of his new coat, just bought for cash at Paragon Sports on Broadway, along with everything else he wore—Irish cable-knit sweater, Merino wool T-shirt, fleece-lined jeans, gloves, watch cap, and hiking boots. Even his socks were new.

The cab pulled away from the curb and Daniel scanned the storefronts across the street. A handcrafted leather goods store, a head shop, a chess store, a dealer of antiquarian maps (est. 1937), and an upscale tattoo parlor. A weathered sign above the chess store read:

MOSCOW RULES ~ CHESS EMPORIUM

Daniel waited for a bearded hipster on a no-brakes fixie to pedal past, then crossed the street. The display window held exquisite hand-crafted chess sets that ran well into the thousands, but also some modest sets and even a plastic ten-dollar magnetic set you could take with your kids on an airplane. He opened the door and stepped inside, pulled off his watch cap, and unzipped the coat.

The store held the full range of sets, boards, pieces, timers, and scoring paraphernalia. The place hadn't seen a renovation in easily over half a century, and it smelled a little dusty. Faded red wallpaper peeled an inch where it met the ceiling.

The young man behind the counter said, "You here to shop, or sit?"

Daniel said, "I'd like to sit."

"That's cool. You looking for a game? I can put your name down."

Daniel shook his head. "I'm just gonna work through some problems."

The kid nodded. "For non-members, I gotta collect the first hour up front."

Daniel peeled a hundred off the wad in his pocket and put it on the counter, Ben Franklin pursing his face at the kid. "I'm gonna park myself for a while. If this runs out, let me know."

The young man stuffed the hundred in his pocket and jerked his chin at the curtained doorway in back.

"Make yourself at home."

The back room was long and narrow, furniture old but solid. Along the wall to Daniel's right stood a row of ten wooden tables, each with a chessboard, a timer, and two chairs. On the left were six similar setups at the back, and a small sitting area up front with two red leather wing chairs and a coffee table laden with chess books and magazines.

Only one table was occupied—a blond ponytailed girl of about ten, her back to the room, playing against a rumpled man in his late sixties who spoke with a thick Russian accent. Daniel shuffled through the magazines on the coffee table while eavesdropping on their game.

The Russian said, "You try your best and you have fun, girl. *Playing* has to be fun; fun can't all hinge on winning."

"It can for me," said the girl. "Winning is fun. Losing sucks donkey balls."

"You're *eleven*, Libby."

"So? Eleven-year-olds aren't all stupid. Losing sucks and winning is fun. That's the way it is. I need to learn to play better so I can win. I don't need the Zen master routine."

"Does your mother know you talk like this?"

"Oh, I'm *way* worse with her." The girl giggled just like a normal eleven-year-old. "Makes her totally crazy."

The Russian shook his head. "You might consider taking it a little easy on the mere mortals in your midst, clever girl. Especially those of us who've taken shits older than you." He moved a chess piece, putting it down with sharp authority. "Let's see you get out of *this* one, Bobby Fischer. And if you *can't* get out of it, count this day as donkey balls." He slapped the button on the timer. "You have thirty minutes to consider your options. Take your time."

Daniel smiled to himself, plucked a magazine off the pile, and sat at a nearby table, facing the curtained doorway, his back to the man and the girl. He flipped through the magazine and stopped on a puzzle that looked interesting, arranging the pieces on the board in front of him to match the illustration on the page.

He didn't really know a chess *problem* from a chess *puzzle*, although he knew there was a difference between the terms. They often had names that sounded like the titles of Cold War thrillers, and chess hobbyists loved to dissect and debate them, but Daniel wasn't into all that. He just enjoyed setting up the board and trying to figure out what he would do if he found himself in such a situation.

He put the magazine aside and examined the options on the board in front of him. He could swap bishop for bishop and gain nothing. He could take both knight and bishop, and gain some real estate with his bishop, but it would cost him his queen. He could lay a trap for Black's rook, but most players would see through it.

Behind him, the Russian said to the girl, "Twenty-five minutes and counting. Remember, it isn't just about how my move has affected your strategic aims. Try to discern what my move reveals about *my* strategic aims. Keep working it. I shall return." He pushed his chair back, walked to the sitting area at the front of the room, and settled into one of the leather wing chairs. He watched as Daniel moved different pieces, reexamined the board, and pulled them back in turn. Each time Daniel auditioned a different move, the Russian let out a dramatic sigh. Finally, he said, "You are a terrible chess player."

"Still learning the game," said Daniel.

"We are all still learning. But you are truly shit at it." The Russian groaned as Daniel pulled back his queen. "Perhaps you should consider checkers."

Daniel put his queen down and looked the man in the eye. "Is this how you prospect for students, Vasili? Because, if you don't mind my saying, you are truly shit at it."

The Russian laughed as he stood and approached the table. "Nonsense, Daniel. Americans love to be abused by a Grandmaster. It makes them feel *legitimate*."

Daniel shook the offered hand. "It's good to see you." He gestured Vasili into the chair opposite.

"I cannot honestly say the same. I had hoped you'd send an envelope for a few years, then a letter saying it was no longer necessary."

"So had I. But it's still good to see you."

Vasili returned the sentiment with a crooked smile. "I thought you had quit the spy game and retired to some undisclosed tropical paradise, trying to die by skin cancer." He nodded at Daniel's face. "Good start on that, by the way."

"Seems the game hasn't quit me."

Vasili looked at Daniel with genuine sadness. "Whatever they're offering you, it isn't enough."

"It wasn't an offer." Daniel dug in his pocket, slid his locker key across the table. "I need it now, Vasili."

The Russian looked at the key but didn't pick it up. "That is so American of you. *Ready! Fire! Aim!* should replace *E pluribus unum*—that one doesn't really fit anymore, if it ever did." A perfunctory laugh at his own joke, and then his face grew serious. "You could've rented a secure locker for a lot less, my friend. You've already paid for my consultation, so at least allow me to consult, before rushing off to your death. You know coming back will draw their fire."

"I'm *already* drawing their fire."

"When?"

"Last night. Two-thirty this morning, actually. And the man they sent is still out there. You know how this works—if I go to ground, they'll just send him again. And they'll send a wetwork team for backup."

"*They?*"

"The Council, probably."

"Probably?"

"They've got the obvious motive."

"But you don't know it's the Council."

"No," Daniel admitted. "I don't know."

"All the more reason to pause. Look at you; you haven't even slept. Your judgment is compromised. You need to get safe and get rest, then consider your options with a clear head. If you don't even know who *they* are, then you can't say with certainty that it wasn't the Foundation who sent the mechanic."

"I'll ask Carter about that when I see him."

Daniel didn't really think Carter Ames was behind the attempt on his life. Carter's Fleur-de-Lis Foundation had put a lot into recruiting him and training him as a field operative. And it had paid off. Daniel's work had enabled the Foundation to stop the Council from doing great harm to the world.

After Daniel killed Conrad Winter and quit the game, Raoul Aharon came to see him in Barbados. Raoul had scouted Daniel for the Foundation, supervised his training, and been his handler. He invited Daniel to take six months of R and R, said to consider it paid leave. Daniel made it clear he had no interest in returning, but Raoul shrugged it off. And the Foundation still put money in Daniel's bank account twice a month.

Clearly, they wanted him back in the fold, and he doubted anybody in Ames's inner circle had gone rogue and ordered a hit on him, but in any organization the size of the Foundation, there would inevitably be factions and power plays. You could count on human nature to rear its ugly head eventually. So he couldn't rule it out completely.

Most likely, the Council for World Peace had sent the gunman. Perhaps they were brewing some new plan to harness AIT, and had decided to take out the guy who stopped them last time before breaking the truce with the Foundation. Or their motive could be as simple as revenge for Conrad Winter's death, to make Daniel an example of what happened if you crossed the line.

Daniel had in fact given the Council plenty of motive, even before he even knew of the Foundation's existence. The Council's top project had been to harness and monopolize the AIT phenomenon, so when Tim Trinity's ability to predict future events became known to the public, they sent Conrad Winter to silence Trinity.

At the time, Daniel had been an investigator for the Vatican's Office of the Devil's Advocate, testing and debunking miracle claims around the world. The Vatican didn't want a Pentecostal televangelist con man leading the world astray, so they sent Daniel to debunk his estranged uncle. But miracle or not, what was happening to Tim Trinity was real. Daniel abandoned the priesthood and dedicated himself to keeping his uncle alive.

Conrad Winter won that battle, and if Daniel had gone on to live the rest of his life as a civilian, the Council would've forgotten all about him. But after being raised by a religious con man, Daniel had spent much of his life searching for God, for proof, and now he'd found . . . something.

A clue to the bigger picture.

So after Tim's death, Daniel joined the Foundation, investigating the AIT phenomenon, searching for answers. And that meant facing off against Conrad Winter and the Council again.

Daniel won that round.

"Vasili, I know what you're gonna say, and I appreciate it, but my needs are a little more immediate. I gotta find the guy who came for me and take him down fast, find out who's behind him. And then I need to climb a rung up the ladder and visit pain upon whoever *that* person is. I'm not rejoining the game, I'm just reestablishing the truce."

"And what if it isn't the Council? What if the Foundation is behind it?"

"Then I need to know that, too."

The Russian shrugged, staring at the key on the table. "Fine. You don't want to listen to reason. But I'm going to tell you a story first, and you are going to hear it."

"Make it brief, I've got somewhere to be."

"Don't get your panties in a knot. This is the story of a man named Gregorovitch—the greatest fighter of wild beasts since King David. His body looked like a drunken subway map, a crisscrossing network of scars, but he never lost a fight. Gregorovitch once killed two black bears with a broken hockey stick. Another time he fought a cougar, using a bowie knife—the cougar ran off so he didn't score a kill that time, but it was still a win, and his streak of wins continued unbroken. He killed a wolverine and a six-foot catfish with his bare hands."

"Not at the same time, I hope."

"Very funny. Gregorovitch held trophy hunters in disdain, said he would never kill an animal without giving the beast a decent chance of killing him. And he chose his weapons accordingly. He became famous, and Russian mobsters got very rich making book on his fights."

Daniel looked at his watch. "I'm gonna die of old age before you get to the punch line, man. I get it: Gregorovitch was a tough, crazy dude, and probably not on the SPCA's Christmas card list."

"Yes, so what happened: A Russian oil billionaire—former high-ranking KGB man—offered Gregorovitch five million Euros to fight an adult male Komodo dragon. Five million, in a Swiss bank account. But it wasn't about the money for Gregorovitch; he wanted to go down in history as the world's greatest beast fighter, wanted to surpass even King David. He spent a week studying every available video of Komodo dragons—fighting each other, attacking humans, hunting prey. He returned to the billionaire and said he would do it, provided he could wear armored boots and gauntlet gloves. And for his weapon, he chose a samurai sword."

"The man had style," said Daniel.

"More style than brains," said Vasili. "A Komodo dragon's mouth is one of the most toxic places on the planet—one bite guarantees a deadly bacterial infection." He caught Daniel's look. "Yes, you knew that. So the billionaire agreed, and a dirt-floor octagon was built in a warehouse outside Riga, seating for two hundred spectators. To get a seat, you had to place a bet of more than one hundred thousand US dollars, and the place was packed like jam. For a bet of ten thousand, you got a password to log in and watch the fight streaming live on the web. Over a thousand people watched online."

Vasili stopped talking.

Daniel said, "*And?*"

"The fight lasted twenty-three seconds. Gregorovitch killed the beast—shoved the samurai sword straight down its throat. But he was bitten, spent his few remaining days in mind-breaking agony as sepsis set in and devoured his body from the inside. Before dying, he only wanted it confirmed that he would go out with an undefeated record, because he outlived the beast."

Vasili picked up the key and stood. "I'll get your kit bag now. But think on it. Whether your assassin was sent by the Foundation or the Council, it doesn't really matter. In either case, there's no way you can go up against them and live. Even if you take out a couple of their top men, what is that to them? Others stand by to pick up the reins. The game isn't just rigged in their favor, Daniel. They own the entire game board. You can't win."

5

It was just before sunrise when the voltage meter beeped in Daniel's hand. Some appliance—toaster oven, coffee maker, or maybe treadmill—had been switched on in the brownstone below. Which meant Carter Ames was up and about, and the interior motion detectors were now switched off.

Daniel uncocooned from the thin metallic emergency blanket, folded it up small, and stowed it back in the kit bag beside him on the rooftop, along with the voltage meter. The windows and doors would still be armed, but he had another gizmo for that.

He stood and stretched his back, looking through the steam clouds of his breath across the rooftops of the neighboring brownstones along East Seventy-Fourth Street, then at the skyscraper skyline to the south. He scooped up the bag, walked to the angled skylight window on his right, and pulled out the other gizmo. It was smaller than a pack of cigarettes. A simple black plastic box with three little green lights on top and a toggle switch on the side, packed with electronic wizardry.

The switch had three positions—Off, Seek, and Send. Daniel switched it to Seek and ran the box slowly around the perimeter of the skylight window's frame, stopping when the tiny green lights came alive. He peeled the waxy tape off the adhesive backing, pressed the unit to the window frame at that exact spot, and held it for a full revolution of his watch's second hand.

Then he switched it to Send.

The lights went dark for less than half a second, then came back on—one, two, three—followed by a quiet beep, confirming that the device was locked on and transmitting.

Four and a half minutes to pick the lock—thinking, *Too slow, out of practice*—and then Daniel had the skylight window open.

He gripped the edge of the window frame and lowered himself into the darkened room, kit bag slung on his back, shoes tied by their laces to his belt, Sig Sauer P232 tucked in his right coat pocket. He extended his arms for the shortest possible drop, then let go, landing soft-footed on the plush padded carpet.

Rich people like their comforts, like their houses quiet. But a quiet house makes for a quiet incursion.

He waited for his eyes to adjust. He was standing in a well-appointed guest bedroom, not recently used. He peeled his gloves off, shoved them in his left pocket, and blew warm air into his cupped hands, bringing them up to room temperature. He reached into his right pocket for the pistol.

Gun in hand, he crept out into the hallway, light filtering up the stairwell from the floor below. Staying tight to the wall, minimizing the creaking underfoot, he walked to the staircase, and down.

On this level he was greeted by the smell of coffee, rising from the kitchen downstairs. Halfway down the hall, a door on the left stood open a few inches. He paused at the door. Inside was the master bedroom, lights on, bed unmade. With his ear to the gap, he could hear the shower running in the en suite master bath.

There would've been a certain satisfaction to walking right in, driving home the point. But it wasn't the smart tactical play. The point was well enough made by the fact that Daniel was in the man's home. Billionaires are not accustomed to having their security breached.

Daniel pulled back from the open door and continued to the end of the hallway, where he stepped into an elegantly furnished study. He closed the door before switching on the lights and placing the pistol on the desk blotter. He put the bag down beside the desk, tossed his hat and coat onto a nearby chair.

A large globe stood in front of a wall of leather-bound books. Daniel lifted the Western Hemisphere and reached for one of the crystal decanters inside. He poured a few fingers of some absurdly expensive Scotch into a tulip snifter, put the snifter on the desk, next to the gun. He untied the shoes from his belt and laced them back on his feet. From his kit bag, he pulled a bottle of spring water. He sat at the desk, poured a tiny splash of water into the Scotch, then took a few deep slugs from the water bottle.

Leaning back in the chair, feeling his body temperature normalize, sipping the whisky, long enough to be confident Carter Ames was out of the shower . . . Daniel lifted the telephone receiver, punched the Intercom button, and then Call All. As he spoke, his voice came out of every speaker in the house.

"Hello, Carter, it's Daniel Byrne. Finish dressing, and come see me at the end of the hall. I'm here to talk—if I'd come to kill you, you'd have died in the shower—so don't press a Panic button and don't bring a gun. I'll know if you do. Just consider this a parley, to which I have rudely invited myself."

Daniel cradled the phone and settled in—he knew Ames would assert what control he could, would not rush. He sipped the Scotch and turned his attention to the large Rothko on the opposite wall.

Two horizontal rectangles with indistinct edges dominated the canvas, the top rectangle—somewhere between orange and red, not quite rust but evoking rust in places—the same width but perhaps half the height of the one below. The larger rectangle was green, but where it was darker it was almost black. The space between the rectangles, and surrounding them to the edge of the canvas, was blue. It was an unhappy image, and it struck Daniel as a sky of fire and blood and rust above a darkening Earth. The smaller rectangle pressing down on the larger. Oppressing.

When the doorknob finally turned, Daniel glanced at his watch: twelve minutes.

Carter Ames entered, every gray hair in place, suit impeccable, right down to the perfect Windsor knot and pocket square.

Ames said, "Bit melodramatic, don't you think?" The transatlantic boarding-school accent was designed to give nothing away. "You could've simply called the office and booked an appointment. We'd have been only too happy to send a plane for you."

Daniel said, "Night before last, a professional tried to take me out."

"We know. We've been waiting for you to check in."

"You know, because . . ."

"We've got cameras on the front and back of your house. We don't look inside, we keep our distance, but we watch. I told you we would look out for you." Ames crossed to the globe bar and poured a drink. "I don't usually take liquor at sunrise, Daniel, and I hope that's not the kind of life you're living in Barbados. Honestly, you don't appear well at all." He looked Daniel in the eye. "How are you feeling these days?"

"I'd feel fine if there weren't an assassin trying to kill me." *Or worse.* But Daniel had decided not to share the gruesome detail of the ECT machine in the back of the van, so that went unspoken for now.

Ames held his dispassionate gaze on Daniel for a moment longer than was comfortable. Finally, he said, "At any rate, our cameras picked up your would-be assassin's approach, and red-flagged our software, which pulled a screen grab clear enough to run through facial recognition."

"Who is he?"

Carter Ames lifted his glass. "One drink to mark the occasion, and then we switch to coffee. I need you sharp." He took a sip. "I am glad you're alive. And glad you've come back, as much as I disapprove of your antagonistic approach."

Daniel gave him the deadeye for a couple seconds before speaking. "Man, give your head a shake. I haven't *come back*. I don't work for you anymore."

"We saved thousands of lives, Daniel. Perhaps hundreds of thousands."

"You're rationalizing."

"You may not like it, but sometimes it really just does come down to the math of the thing. We killed a couple of hundred while saving many times that number. If we could've saved those people, we would have."

"Bullshit. You could've convinced your allies in the military to mount a rescue operation." Daniel sipped his scotch. "They were civilian hostages. They deserved at least that."

"You know we couldn't," said Carter Ames. "Not without—"

"—revealing your existence to the world, I know."

Ames sat in a leather chair by the coffee table. "This is exactly why I had Raoul remove you from the operation."

Daniel's laugh came bitter from his mouth. "So it wasn't about reading-in Kara at all. You didn't have time to argue with me, so you benched me."

"And you responded by killing Conrad, against my explicit orders." Before Daniel could reply, Ames said, "My point is, we both did something the other didn't approve of."

Daniel placed his drink on the desk blotter, beside the pistol. "I put a mass murderer out of business. You ordered a goddamned drone strike on 263 innocents. These things are not morally equivalent." He knew he should shut up, but this needed to be said. "And in a few months, America will have a hundred thousand troops back in the Middle East. Boots on the ground in active combat, because the world thinks Yemeni Islamists carried out a bioweapon attack in South Carolina. But somehow, by your calculus, the Foundation's anonymity is more important than telling the world what really happened and stopping that war. How's your math gonna look after you factor in the coming body count?"

Carter Ames said, "The Foundation does not reveal itself, full stop. Revealed, we could no longer operate in the world with any real power. If we fail to remain in the game, we cannot continue to influence the future, and we cede control to those who do not flinch at atrocity. For God's sake, you saw what the Council did in Liberia; you know what they would've done to those hostages, had they gotten away. Regardless, we do not reveal ourselves, and *that's* the bottom line. So we shall simply have to agree to disagree, and move forward. Re-litigating the past is not productive."

"Then stop trying to recruit me. I'm not coming back."

After a moment, Ames nodded. "If you change your mind, let me know. As a Foundation operative, you'd be under our protection, and there *is* a man trying to kill you."

"Faulty logic," said Daniel. "When last we spoke, you told me a truce on AIT had been reached—"

"Indeed, and all indicators tell us the truce remains in place. The Council continues to compete with us over the cases of AIT that occur by . . . well, by nature. But they have made no further attempt to deploy the bacterium that can trigger AIT."

"Which still leaves revenge for Conrad's death as a perfectly viable motive," said Daniel. "But you told me a condition of that truce was the Council not putting a target on me. So I was already supposed to be under your protection. Either the Council has broken the terms of your truce, or someone inside your organization wants me dead badly enough to betray you."

"Those are the most obvious possibilities. Which is why I imme-diately put the IT team to the task of building a profile on the man who came after you. And I can tell you for a fact, he has no link to either the Council or the Foundation." Ames put his drink on the coffee table and stood up. "Now if you'd like to see the file, kindly put the pistol away and get us some coffee."

6
=

Carter Ames collected the pages as his printer spat them out, scanning the top page while he added the others behind it. "The man who tried to kill you is Lucien Drapeau."

An abandoned New Orleans housing project flashed in Daniel's mind. Racing up the stairs to the sun-blistered rooftop, ducking bullets, scrambling around the corner of the building, hanging onto window ledges, swinging himself back up onto the roof . . . aiming, squeezing the trigger.

He said, "That's not possible. I—"

Ames raised his hand. "You killed Drapeau, I know." He sipped his coffee. "Lucien Drapeau is the highest-paid assassin in the Western Hemisphere—just think of the name not as a name but as a title. You killed the previous Lucien Drapeau. This man is his successor."

He handed the top sheet to Daniel. A vital statistics summary—height, weight, eye color, hair color—along with a headshot that looked like a passport photo. It was the man who had twice tried to kill Daniel . . . once in a meditation-induced AIT vision and once in real life.

"The Drapeau legend is managed by a blue-chip law firm in Montreal. They keep several former PMs and cabinet ministers on the masthead, and their clients span the globe. But Drapeau isn't just a hit man for international business; he does wetwork for the intelligence community, organized crime, wealthy jealous husbands. Drapeau and his managers at the firm are completely agnostic; they'll take just about any client who can pay the fee, which is reputed to be over ten million dollars per contract. In essence, he's a hit man for the *one percent*."

Daniel said, "Pat told me about the last Drapeau. Said clients know the man can be trusted not to talk—that comes with the fee—but they can't expect ongoing loyalty. You could hire him to take out your business partner, and a week later your partner's grieving widow could hire him to take you out."

Ames smiled. "Sounds like Pat. Perhaps a tad overstated, but essentially true. That's the reputation, anyhow. As you well know, with the games we play and the stakes for which we play them, loyalty is the essential currency, the very bedrock on which we stand. Without it, we could not exist. And the same is true for our adversaries. I would not think so little of the Council to even consider that they would do business on such a basis. They're far too smart for that. We must conclude that someone else entirely has decided to end your life. And that person has hired the very best."

"So it would appear," said Daniel.

Ames squared the remaining pages on the table. "This new Lucien Drapeau first appears forty-five days after the death of his predecessor, just after leaving a luxury private plastic surgery clinic in Cartagena. His appearance does not coincide with the disappearance of any elite assassins known to us, but he may have popped up from the military, paramilitary, just about anywhere." He fixed Daniel with a long look. "We're positively awash in skilled, nihilistic assassins these days. Sign of the times, I'm afraid. At any rate, we don't know who he was before he became Drapeau, and we don't even know his original nationality. Our earliest hit on facial recognition was his arrival at Montreal's Dorval Airport, post-surgery, just off a flight from JFK, originating in Colombia." He handed another page across.

It was a security camera image of Drapeau standing at the immigration counter, speaking with the border agent. Not a high-resolution image, but the Foundation's computer geeks had cleaned it up and Daniel could just make out the thin pink line in front of the ear, leading down under the jaw, the subtle discoloration still fading around the eyes and at the sides of the nose, all of which had been digitally removed from the passport photo.

"He's had cheek implants," said Daniel. "And his jaw line reshaped."

"And a nose job, and something with his brow, and although I can't see it from this angle, I'd wager he's also had his ears reshaped. There's no way we can extrapolate his original face." Ames sipped some coffee. "So we've devoted a great deal of computing power to tracking this face. Wherever he hangs his hat is off the grid. A few months ago, he pops up here in Manhattan, staying at the Grand Hyatt for six days. Eats at the Grand Central Oyster Bar and the Four Seasons, but dines alone. Drinks at the Rum House at the Edison on West Forty-Seventh—no camera coverage in the bar, but we scanned faces entering and exiting the hotel during his times there, found no persons of interest."

Ames handed two more pages to Daniel. "During Drapeau's stay in town, an SEC investigator died of a slip-and-fall in the bathtub, and a particularly dirty hedge fund manager shot himself in the head. But we have no idea if Drapeau was behind either, both, or neither."

Daniel looked at the accompanying photographs and vital statistics of the two dead men, recognizing neither their faces nor their names. "What else have you got?"

"We've got him in London for four days, during which time a banker who handled UK investments for some very bad Russian and Chinese billionaires died of a heart attack while in the company of a lady of the evening, and a Saudi prince overdosed on heroin. Again, we don't know if there's a connection to Drapeau, but if he was in London on a contract, these are his two most likely targets."

Daniel examined the pages. Nothing.

"No other potential assassinations since London," Ames continued, "but Drapeau did travel a great deal for meetings, popping up in DC, Montreal, Dallas, Las Vegas, Barcelona, Istanbul, Moscow."

"Anything connecting his contacts?"

"Other than their wealth? Not particularly. All known associates are not only members of the one percent—they're members of the one tenth of one percent. The barons of various industries. Finance, media, fossil fuels, military and intelligence, international arms sales, organized crime, politics. All plausible clients, but nothing that connects to AIT, or to you."

"Okay, what else?"

"Drapeau visited New Orleans." He held Daniel's eye. "He was in your hometown for ten days, Daniel."

Daniel shrugged. "Basic due diligence—he'd build a profile on me, look for my patterns and weaknesses before making his approach."

"And he came straight to you in Barbados, where you were supposed to be living under the radar. But there has been no probing—no attempt whatsoever—to test the Ian Shefras legend. Our systems would've caught it. It seems Drapeau's client already knew where to find you."

Ian Shefras was the new identity the Foundation had created for Daniel, and it should've been bulletproof, even if probed. It came complete with birth records, a Social Security number, school transcripts from kindergarten through college, tax records going back ten years, credit cards, a passport—the works. A full paper trail, for anyone who looked. The people in Barbados who knew Daniel knew him as Ian, a laid-back business consultant who'd sold his company and retired young, living off his investments—just another expat in paradise. But if there'd been no attempt to probe the identity, then Ames was right: Drapeau's client must've already known where Daniel was hanging his hat.

Ames took another long sip of coffee. "You were extremely lucky to get away once; he won't miss a second time. Our door remains open to you. Step through it, and we'll protect you while we find this man."

Daniel shook his head.

"Very well." Ames put his cup back in its saucer. "It's your funeral."

"You can use the money you keep dumping in my account to throw me a good send-off. Open bar, canapés, a brass band for the second line."

"Don't be childish." Ames glanced at the remaining pages in his hand. "You will come back to us, Daniel. And when you do, you will want to, or at least need to. But until then, Drapeau is your problem, and the Foundation will not devote any further attention to the problems of an outsider. I do hope you survive to come back, and toward that end, I'm sharing what we've learned. But after you leave here this morning, you are on your own. Understood?"

"Understood."

Ames handed the pages across. "We've got twelve known associates for Drapeau, none connected in any way to the Council or the Foundation."

Daniel looked at the first page. A man in his sixties—petroleum lobbyist in Washington, face and name unfamiliar. The second page was a Montreal lawyer named Eric Murphy. Handsome, trim, late fifties.

Ames said, "We believe Murphy is Drapeau's manager at the firm. They've twice met for lunch at the Ritz-Carlton."

Daniel flipped through the pages. He recognized the media baron, as would most, and a few of the other faces, as would any reader of the *Economist*, the *Wall Street Journal*, *Forbes*, or *Wired*. They were superstars of their respective worlds. But Daniel could see no reason any of them would even know of his existence, much less want him dead.

The next page was a photo of Drapeau sitting with a redheaded man at an outdoor café. The man wore large sunglasses with mirrored lenses.

"That was taken in Barcelona," said Ames. "We have no idea who the other man is."

Daniel flipped to the final page and his heart jumped in his chest. He was staring into the face of the woman from his vision. It was an enlargement of a Spanish driver's license. The name on the license: Dana Cameron.

The voice in his head belonged to this woman.

Daniel said, "Who's Dana Cameron?" It required some effort to keep his tone neutral.

"An American, professor of archeology, she's been at the University of Barcelona almost seven years. She researches, lectures, publishes papers on her excursions. Cameron is a civilian, earns a professor's salary, no connection to anything that we can see. Just an archeologist from New England."

New England. The accent matched. So the voice in Daniel's head belonged to a woman who existed as a real person, in real life. The thought made him dizzy.

He put it away for later. "She's just a civilian, what's her connection to Drapeau?"

"We don't know. He entered Spain under the name Larry Elias in the morning, met the man with the sunglasses for a café lunch, and then visited Dr. Cameron's office, signing in at reception with his alias. He exited the building twenty minutes later and departed the country the same night." Ames drank the last of his coffee, put the cup in the saucer, and stood. "And now that I've told you what we've learned, our assistance is at an end."

Daniel stood and shrugged into his coat, picked up his kit bag. "Thanks for sharing, Carter. Have a nice day."

Ames waited until Daniel was at the door, then said, "One more thing. If you ever again approach me with a gun in your hand, I will have you killed."

Daniel stopped and turned. Without changing his expression at all, Ames let him see the hard man behind the urbane façade, just for a moment, and then put it away again. Nice trick.

Daniel said, "If I ever again approach you with a gun in my hand, it won't be to talk." He pointed up, toward the rooftop skylight through the ceiling. "And by the way, I just flagged the hole in your security apparatus. I did you a favor. But no need to thank me. You're welcome."

Carter Ames didn't smile, but his face softened ever so slightly.

"Survive to come back, Daniel. Good hunting."

7
=

Daniel squinted at the late-afternoon sun reflecting off the ocean's surface. The sun that never moved. He stood barefoot on the beach, his pants rolled into loose cuffs just below his knees.

Dana Cameron stood facing him, smiling as her hair whipped wild in the warm wind. She wore a faded red T-shirt with a yellow lightning bolt in a white circle—the logo of the Flash—and a long blue beach wrap. She wiggled her toes in the sand.

Daniel said, "You like the Flash?"

She nodded, her grin widening. "The question is: Does the Flash move very quickly, or does he slow time?" She pushed her glasses up her nose. "Anyway, time is just how we experience change, and *forward* is how we experience entropy, so in our reality time appears to move forward—but according to physics, our experience of the passage of time is just an illusion."

"Okay but without the riddles, please," said Daniel. "What are you trying to tell me?"

Dana Cameron pointed at Daniel's feet. "Wiggle your toes."

✦ ✦ ✦

Daniel started awake under sweat-soaked sheets, his mouth still burning with the taste of cinnamon, forehead cold and clammy, headache raging, heart pounding against his ribs.

Sunlight fought its way into the room through a gap in the drapes. The bedside clock read 2:56 p.m.

He untangled himself from the sheets, walked shivering to the thermostat, and cranked the heat. Flipped on the bathroom light, fumbled through his dopp kit, and managed to pour a couple of BC headache powders onto his tongue without spilling much. He filled a glass at the sink and poured water in and around his mouth and got the bitter powder down. He shivered his way over to the tub, spun the shower on hot.

Just a rush, an excess of adrenaline. That's all it was, but his nervous system was flirting with fight-or-flight. If he didn't calm it down, he'd soon be having tunnel vision.

This happened sometimes after an AIT dream. Neurological panic, without a mental counterpart. Daniel didn't imagine bad guys were about to burst into the hotel room, or that he was having a heart attack, or anything that would trigger such an adrenaline rush. Still, his heart pounded and the hair on his forearms stood up. His scalp tingled and perspiration poured from him. He felt hypothermic.

He stepped into the steaming shower without even trying to fumble out of his shorts and sat down in the tub, shivering under the hot spray.

✤ ✤ ✤

Daniel marched up Lexington Avenue, keeping his speed up, giving the adrenaline somewhere to go. The rush had eased while he sat in the hot shower, stabilized as he dressed. But it needed some help to normalize. He could still taste cinnamon.

He wore dark sunglasses and his watch cap pulled down over his ears to dampen the sensory input. Still, the world was uncomfortably bright and loud and smelly, and he was too aware of the fabric of his clothes touching his skin.

It was not enough to be able to enter the vision on purpose—he also had to be able to *not* enter the vision when it came calling uninvited. With an assassin on his case in the real world, the timing might not always be convenient.

The timing wasn't actually inconvenient now—he'd been safely ensconced in an upscale hotel, locked in his room, checked in under the name Colin Silvester. He needed to resist it now simply to learn *how* to resist it.

A skill that might save his life; the sooner acquired, the better.

So he would march up Lex at this pace, and if the rush decreased sufficiently, he would stop for dinner at the Grand Hyatt. Alcohol would help settle his nervous system, but he would limit himself to four drinks, over a couple of hours, with food. He would be careful not to overcompensate. He didn't want to dampen the senses too much, just in case.

There was no reason to think Lucien Drapeau could've tracked him to New York. Daniel had traveled from Barbados as Colin Silvester on a passport not even the Foundation knew about. Only two other people knew of its existence—Yoshi Inoue, the forger who made it, and Pat Wahlquist, Daniel's best friend.

Though extraordinarily slim, there was still a chance the assassin could be in New York by coincidence. In which case, he'd avoid any bars and hotels and restaurants he'd spent time in on his last visit. Hence, the Grand Hyatt. Drapeau had spent more time there than any other place in the file; it would be the last place in Manhattan he'd want to be, were he in town.

After leaving Carter Ames and checking into his hotel, Daniel had used his computer to send Pat a voice-mail. He had no doubt that Pat would reply with an invitation to visit, and he was betting the invitation would be in his voice-mail inbox when he returned to his room.

This surety allowed Daniel to take this walk, but he still felt twitchy as hell, his gait was too stiff, and he considered the possibility that perhaps he should've settled for jumping jacks and Hindu squats in his room. Crossing Thirty-Eighth Street, he guessed he'd have to walk a dozen blocks past the Hyatt, and back, before he could sit still. Then he realized the cinnamon taste was no longer waning, but was in fact getting stronger.

Oh. Shit.

A violent electric current ran through Daniel's nervous system and his knees buckled, his stumble drawing contemptuous looks from a couple of passing businessmen.

And then she spoke. The woman from his visions, this archeologist from New England, her voice coming from everywhere at once, filling his head. "Daniel, pay attention. I can help you, but I need you to come back. You have to cross over."

A new shudder rocked him—his shoulders and arms twitched and he wobbled slightly but didn't stumble.

One of the men called out, "Go sleep it off, douchebag."

Dana Cameron's disembodied *voice-of-god* voice said, "Your life is in danger."

"Jesus Christ," Daniel cut in, "you think I don't know that?" He had no reason to believe she could hear him—the voice in his head had never responded to his attempts at conversation before—but he knew he couldn't contain himself, knew his mouth had to speak it. So he would act the part of an agitated man in the midst of a strange phone call.

As he lifted his phone to his ear, Dana Cameron's voice said, "You need to cross over and find me here. Over a thousand lives will be lost. I've seen it."

Will be.

"So this," Daniel blurted, "this event you've been warning me about is in the future. When?"

Her voice again: "Just let go of where you are, and wake up here."

The world lost its mooring. Lexington Avenue started revolving around Daniel, then sped up, and his last terrible thought before passing out was:

This is what it feels like to go right out of your gourd.

8

Sound returned first.

Tree frogs?

No.

Electronic.

Beeping.

For a while, sound was all—long enough for Daniel to identify it as the sound of a heart monitor. Then the antiseptic smell—hospital—followed by body awareness—lying in a hospital bed—and finally—at last—he became aware of light behind his eyelids, and he opened his eyes.

A man stood at the foot of Daniel's bed. Daniel blinked him into focus. Average height, fighter's physique, swarthy.

Raoul Aharon. Mossad, years ago, before joining the Foundation. He'd been Daniel's handler, martial arts instructor, and chief ball-buster.

Raoul nodded. "Dorothy awakes."

"Always fancied myself more of a Sleeping Beauty," said Daniel.

Raoul stepped closer. "Enjoy the ride?"

Daniel said, "How long was I out?"

"Just over four hours since you collapsed in the street. Someone calls 9-1-1, ambulance brings you to Bellevue, no ID, your face goes into the system as a John Doe, and you pop up on our screens about twenty-three minutes after EMS picked you up. I've been standing watch ever since."

Daniel found the button to raise his bed up to sitting, waited until the electric motor clicked off. "But I'm an outsider now, so why is my passing out in the street of interest to you?"

Raoul made his exasperation clear with his whole face, backing it up with a sound not unlike a growl. "I know you're not coming back, Daniel, but when you *do* come back, I will take great joy, kicking your ass all over the mats. You'll shed some blood for all the bullshit you're putting us through. Sneaking up on Carter was not okay."

Daniel smiled. "Sorry I made you look a fool in front of the boss. But I didn't design his security, I just walked through the hole you guys left in it. So get over your own bad self." He sat upright and turned, swinging his feet out of the bed, reached for the cart and shut off the damn beeping, then pulled the pulse finger-clamp thing off his finger. "I'm gonna check myself out. And when I leave, I'm leaving alone. So if you're here for a reason, now's the time."

Raoul combed his fingers through his curly hair, blew out a long breath, holding back his first response. He said, "Doctor needs to speak with you before you leave, to be sure you haven't suffered a mental breakdown. You were behaving erratically before you passed out. They've ruled out stroke and epilepsy, and aside from an insignificant amount of alcohol, they found no intoxicants in your system."

Daniel said, "I can tell you what they found. They found a titanic dose of caffeine, elevated stress hormones, depleted adrenaline, and you know what else?" He eyed the IV line running from the back of his left hand up to the saline bag hanging above. "I'm dehydrated." He looked back to Raoul. "I went from tropical heat to below freezing, no sleep for forty-six hours, mainlining coffee. I acted erratically because I was battling not to lose consciousness on Lexington Avenue. I was trying to push through it."

Raoul nodded impatiently. "Of course, that's exactly what you'll tell them, and they'll believe you. But I know what really went down. I do. You had an episode. You've got AIT."

"Are you high?" said Daniel.

Raoul continued as if Daniel hadn't spoken. "I'm actually jealous. Seriously, I'd give my left nut to be one of the chosen. A conduit to God?" He shrugged. "Or the little grouchy guy pulling levers behind the curtain—whatever we choose to call whatever's behind the veil."

"Raoul. Stop. I don't have AIT."

Daniel held Raoul's eye, counted seven Mississippis before Raoul said, "No shit?"

"No shit," Daniel lied.

"Oh." Raoul was quiet for a few seconds. "Then you better get ready, my friend, because you will."

In the depths of his mind, Daniel had known it was coming for longer than he was comfortable admitting. From the sheer coincidence of being sent by the Vatican to debunk his own long-estranged uncle, to the physical impossibility of Tim speaking backward and predicting the future—each time Daniel had found himself facing a crack in reality, almost catching a glimpse of something beyond what we know, and each time it hit like vertigo, almost like the feeling of slipping into or out of an AIT vision.

There had been so many times with his uncle. And the soldier in West Virginia had known Daniel had been a priest. And all the impossible coincidences that had put Julia's Air Force Intelligence file with Michael Dillman's name in his hands . . . the impossibility of opening Kara's journal—one of a hundred, selected at random—letting it fall open to a random page and finding the exact same phrase spoken by the AIT-stricken American soldier. Ignoring the impossibility of the phrase being in both places, Daniel was the only person on Earth who had heard the soldier speak those words—the only person who could've recognized them in Kara's journal.

And then there was Angelica Ory in New Orleans. Tim had seen her in an AIT vision. Although they were strangers, he woke from the vision with her name and her French Quarter address in his head. When Daniel and Tim walked into her place, she took one look at Daniel and dropped her teacup. She had dreamed of Daniel, not Tim.

AIT had been repeatedly pointing its creepy finger at Daniel, and he'd chosen to ignore it. But looking deep into his sense of self, he knew it went back even further. Somehow, it had always been there, like the softest whisper of wind in his mind's ear.

But AIT was no longer just pointing at Daniel. Now it had him by the throat, and he could no longer afford to ignore anything.

The question was: How did *Raoul* know Daniel was going to get AIT? But the answer to that question would come at the price of Daniel coming in from the cold. That was the carrot Raoul dangled, but to bite it Daniel would have to admit he had AIT, and he was damned if he'd serve the Foundation as a guinea pig.

He said, "It doesn't run in families, you know that. My uncle having had AIT doesn't increase my odds. Hell, maybe *you're* gonna get it next, and you can keep both your nuts."

"Daniel, you're not hearing me. We don't suspect you're going to get AIT, we know it. It's why we scouted you in the first place." Raoul waved his hand around in a small circle. "You say you don't have it, and I admit I can't tell if you're lying. We trained you too well. But if you're not, then it just hasn't hit you yet. Maybe this event was the first blip—the arrival may be imminent. But sooner or later, AIT is coming for you, and you don't want to go through it alone. You'll need our help."

Daniel put his bare feet on the cold linoleum, pushed himself to standing, and found he was steady on his feet. He grabbed the IV stand by its pole and dragged it along with him as he shuffled across the room. "Thanks for stopping by, Raoul. If at some future date I start speaking in tongues and I want your help with that, I'll be in touch. Meanwhile, I gotta piss like a racehorse."

Raoul shook his head. "You don't have to be quite so much of an asshole."

"Apparently," said Daniel, "I do have to be at least this much of an asshole. Do I need to have it tattooed on my forehead? Not. Coming. Back." Daniel opened the door and gestured to the hallway.

"Right," said Raoul as he left the room. "Good luck with that."

9
=

I t's staggering," said Anderson Cooper, looking up from the copy of *The Truth (So Far) about Trinity* that lay on the anchor desk to his right, "how much has changed in such a short time." He swiveled to face Julia Rothman. "When you first appeared on the show, we were both convinced Tim Trinity's predictions were fraudulent, that he was running some kind of con job on the world."

Julia chuckled. "To be fair, Trinity was, by his own admission, a con man—he said so on national television. And he was predicting the future—something we still don't understand—so extreme skepticism was reasonable. Extraordinary claims demand extraordinary proof—I said at the time, we have to follow the evidence where it leads and resist the urge to get ahead of ourselves."

"And you've been following the evidence ever since. What do we now know, for sure, that we didn't then?"

"We know that what happened to Tim Trinity was a real phenomenon—scientists now studying it are using the term Anomalous Information Transfer. Trinity really did predict future events that were impossible to know ahead of time, with one hundred percent accuracy. And we know this AIT phenomenon is happening to other people."

"But we still don't know what AIT is, or where this anomalous information is coming from."

"No, we don't."

"Tim Trinity thought God was speaking to him."

Julia nodded. "He was completely convinced of it, thought the predictions were God's way of drawing the world's attention so he could deliver God's message."

"Which was basically, 'Be nice to each other.'"

"Basically, yes. *Do unto others as you would have them do unto you.* He called it 'God's only commandment.' But that's the central tenet of almost every religion you can name—it seems dubious to me that, after all these years, God would finally reveal himself just to say something that every religion already ascribes to him. Despite Trinity's certainty, we don't even know if there is a god, much less knowing that God is causing AIT."

"In the book, you write about six cases of AIT, and you profile three in depth. None of them share Trinity's belief."

"Right. Of the three, one is an atheist, one is a Zen Buddhist who also doesn't believe in a supreme being, and one is a lapsed Catholic who dabbles in voodoo and says he has no idea what to believe. All three are now working with university neurologists and psychologists and parapsychologists, and we'll just have to stay tuned and see what further evidence they uncover. One thing's for sure: We're living in strange times."

Cooper shook his head. "People are not reacting well to these strange times, to put it mildly. They're angry. Look at these scenes, going on just today."

The television screen filled with footage of demonstrations around the world, people with raised fists and bullhorns marching past parliaments and capitol buildings, gathering in public squares, in front of churches and mosques and temples.

Some carried signs proclaiming the arrival of the End Times or salvation—or both—but most carried signs of simple protest.

HOW MANY HAVE AIT?
STOP THE LIES
WHAT IS THE REAL NUMBER?
TELL US THE TRUTH
THE PUBLIC HAS A RIGHT TO KNOW

Over the protest footage, Cooper said, "Almost eighty thousand demonstrators in St. Peter's Square, forty thousand in Washington, DC, twenty in Paris, over thirty in Berlin and Tokyo, twenty-five in Moscow . . . every major city around the globe, and growing fast. Authorities are expecting a massive protest at next month's emergency G7 meeting in London."

The screen cut back to the studio set. Cooper said, "These people believe there's a conspiracy of silence. They think the people in power are not telling all they know about AIT, what it is and how far it has spread."

Julia let out a wry grin. "In my experience, people in power rarely tell all they know, about anything. And not just people in power—most people don't tell all they know. As a journalist, I have to accept that reality and get on with my job, keep digging. Several doctors studying AIT have estimated that there are perhaps a few thousand cases worldwide, but like everyone, my sources have their own agendas, and I suspect many more than a few thousand. I'm not trying to feed conspiracy theories, but I think people are angry for a reason. I don't think we're being told everything."

"How many more cases do you suspect?"

"I just don't know yet. That's why my book is called *The Truth (So Far)*."

Cooper said, "Protest organizers are pointing to the worldwide spike in admissions to psychiatric hospitals and mental health clinics as evidence that AIT is far more widespread than authorities are admitting. At least two hundred thousand more psychiatric admissions than the same month last year, as estimated by the World Health Organization."

"It's true there is a spike," conceded Julia, "but we can't jump to the conclusion that these are cases of AIT. Some may be, but most are probably not. We're living in a time of high anxiety on many fronts— Brexit, the bioterror attack in South Carolina, widening war in the Middle East, the election, the economy, increased droughts and the effects of climate change . . . many mental health professionals believe the cumulative weight of recent world events could easily explain the mental health crisis we're seeing."

Cooper said, "Protest leaders also point out that a disturbing number of these people are claiming the end of the world is imminent."

Julia smiled. "Social media feeds our conspiracy culture, and I think that's been blown out of proportion. Look at it this way: With Tim Trinity and AIT, our concept of reality took a hit. People began asking the big questions again—questions of a metaphysical nature. For most, that means questions of a religious nature. The top three religions in the world—Christianity, Islam, and Hinduism—all predict an apocalyptic future for humanity, so it's not unreasonable to assume that people raised in these belief systems who are now experiencing a mental health crisis would come to believe that Trinity and all the other anxiety factors are signs of the apocalypse. But Tim Trinity himself did not predict an apocalypse, and neither has any other *confirmed* AIT sufferer, as far as we know."

"Bullshit," muttered a man's voice from down the bar. Daniel ignored it.

Julia was saying, "Just as nature abhors a vacuum, human nature abhors an information vacuum. In the absence of information, con-spiracy theories thrive and spread on social media, driving the public closer to panic. It's too late to keep AIT quiet, and continued secrecy doesn't seem to be serving the public good."

Daniel felt a slight pang of guilt in his gut as she looked straight into the camera and added, "I'm optimistic that someone who knows more about AIT will be moved by the public protests to check their moral compass, and will see the need to come forward."

But Daniel had told Julia what he could, and guilt wasn't pro-ductive. The non-disclosure agreement he'd signed upon joining the Fleur-de-Lis Foundation had been a symbolic gesture. If he passed the Foundation's secrets to a journalist, they wouldn't sue him, they'd just end him. One of the downsides of getting involved with the shadow world of billionaire power brokers and the secret games they play.

"Complete load of bullshit."

"Tell me about it."

Daniel turned from the television to the two men down the bar to his right. Slightly drunk business travelers, midwestern accents, one maybe twenty-eight, the other maybe forty, both wearing midrange suits, cheap haircuts, and expensive watches.

The younger one said, "I mean, Julia *Rothman*, right? Probably a mouthpiece for the Illuminati, part of the cover-up. Shoveling disinformation so we don't find out who's really behind AIT."

The older one said, "She could be and not even know it, the way they control corporate lamestream media. Twitter's the only real journalism left."

Daniel turned away from the idiots, took a deep breath, and let it out. The way the younger man had leaned into Julia's surname made Daniel want to hit him, but getting arrested at JFK was not part of a winning survival strategy. He rattled the ice in his drink, held the cold glass against his temple to ease the headache now coming on.

He tossed back the rest of his drink and signaled the bartender for the check, as the headache grew constant, like a weather headache.

Like an AIT headache.

Was that cinnamon he tasted in the background, peeking out from behind the amber rum? Or was he just imagining it, looking for it and fearing it at the same time? He couldn't tell.

Jesus.

Being in an assassin's crosshairs sucked donkey balls, to use Chess Girl's expression, but at least it was a problem to be dealt with. Dealing with it while losing his mind, however, was proving a challenge.

Before Drapeau arrived with his van of horrors, Daniel had been progressing, gaining some control of his AIT. Now he felt completely out of control, of everything. The memory of blinking out on

Lexington Avenue arose in Daniel unbidden—the feeling of utter helplessness, as control slipped away—and for a moment, he felt untethered in space and time.

Damn it.

Daniel hadn't had an AIT vision after passing out on the street. AIT visions were not like normal dreams, which are sometimes forgotten upon awakening only to surface in memory later. Every time Daniel had been hit with AIT while asleep, he'd awakened with the vision in the forefront of his mind.

So Daniel had successfully resisted AIT, but at the cost of passing out in the street. And with an assassin on his tail, that represented no survival advantage.

Before he'd lost consciousness, Dana Cameron's voice had told him to *cross over*, which suggested that she could enter and exit the vision at will, presumably without passing out. Perhaps she could teach him how.

She'd also warned him—not for the first time—of a devastated city with many dead. And this time, she'd spoken of it in the future tense. Was this coming event connected with Lucien Drapeau?

Daniel had only had one drink at the airport bar but it felt like four, and this line of thinking was not helping to quell his growing sense of unreality.

Change the channel in your head. Now.

Daniel dropped too much money on the bar and got out of there in a hurry. He stopped near his gate and rented time at an iPad kiosk, where he directed the browser to the news site of the *Barbados Advocate*, searching for normalcy.

Top story: The prime minister was hosting a celebratory dinner, honoring the men's and women's West Indies cricket teams, both of which had recently become world champions. Nice.

After reinventing himself in Barbados as Ian Shefras, Daniel had taken in a few cricket matches at Kensington Oval. Though he'd fought in Golden Gloves as a teen and still watched boxing on TV occasionally, his heart belonged to baseball. People who don't like cricket often complain of the length and pace of the game, something baseball fans are used to hearing from those sad souls who have no baseball love in their hearts, so he thought he might enjoy cricket.

He was wrong. He found the game unfathomable, couldn't get into it. What he loved, and what he returned for, was the social scene at the Oval. The characters and costumes, the betting and banter, the music of Mac Fingall and his band.

Despite coping with the voices and visions in his head, the nightmares and adrenaline rushes and lost sleep, Daniel had been optimistic in that life. The spy game behind him, focusing not on power plays and politics, but on the phenomenon he was experiencing.

Focusing on the here and now, with hope for a future, maybe even a future with Kara.

He had to get back to that.

Had to.

Daniel tapped on the iPad to bring up the next story.

A large crane had toppled over on the building site of a new five-star resort, crushing two bungalows still under construction and ripping the front wall off a larger completed building. Seven workers had been taken to Queen Elizabeth Hospital with moderate to serious injuries. The Minister of Labor had appeared before reporters to announce the launch of an accident investigation by Occupational Safety and Health.

Daniel moved on to the next story. It brought a welcome smile.

A coalition of Bajan church ladies had released a statement expressing disapproval of Rihanna's latest antics and urging the government to allocate funds for promoting moral rectitude among the island's youth. Meanwhile, the island's youth were celebrating the news that Rihanna would be coming home for a concert to coincide with next year's Crop Over festival.

Maybe Daniel would see the show, if he made it to the next year alive and halfway sane.

10
==

Planters Inn—Savannah, Georgia

*T*oday is a good day to die. But I've decided to stay alive until tomorrow.

Daniel ended his meditation with the phrase he'd learned in the Foundation's dojo, as he had every morning since his training.

He opened his eyes and stood from zazen, then went through his katas in the spacious hotel room, took a quick shower, and sat on the canopied bed, his laptop in front of him, a borrowed atlas serving as a lap desk.

On the screen, a web page displayed text transcriptions of his voice-mails. He had a Digicel wireless account—a 246 number assigned to Ian Shefras, the Foundation-created identity Daniel had lived under in Barbados. He'd destroyed the phone before leaving the island, and the SIM card was now traveling the world on perpetual tour, tucked under the upholstery of seat 4C in a Delta Airlines Boeing 777. But the number lived on, account paid, and the voice-mail still functioned. Accessing it was a manageable risk.

Daniel was connected to the web through multiple levels of encryption and anonymizers. Even if Drapeau or his employer were watching, and even if they were willing to devote a shit-ton of computing power to the task, by the time the trail of electronic breadcrumbs pointed here, Daniel would be out of the country.

Accessing the voice-mails themselves was an even taller order for a hypothetical intruder. If you had a facsimile of Daniel's thumbprint and also got by the password, then you'd see an empty voice-mail box. The Foundation's geeks had hacked Digicel and installed a software patch, making the account status constantly refresh as NRA—No Recent Activity. You'd have to then click through into an apparently empty mailbox to discover that emptiness can be an illusion.

Daniel placed his thumb on the laptop's pad, then typed his current password. This would be the last time he'd send a message from this account. He'd still be able to check for messages, but sending was the bigger risk. Once he got to Europe, he'd pick up pay-as-you-go phones to send messages, and burn them frequently.

There was a new voice-mail from Kara. He hadn't yet responded to her previous message, left three days ago, when she had suggested they get together for a weekend and catch up. He'd planned to reply the next morning and invite her to visit in a couple of weeks, but Lucien Drapeau scuttled that plan when he showed up in the middle of the night.

Kara's voice-mails showed on the screen as coming from a phone belonging to Maya Seth.

Because Kara Singh was officially dead.

Conrad Winter had, on behalf of the Council for World Peace, sunk a blade between her ribs. She'd flatlined, almost died, but not quite. In order to keep her invisible to the Council, the Foundation pulled some strings, simultaneously killing an American doctor named Kara Singh and creating a Canadian doctor named Maya Seth. This, shortly after Daniel Byrne had disappeared amid the chaos of a plague outbreak in South Carolina . . . and Ian Shefras first appeared in Barbados.

Life gets complicated.

Daniel and Kara had recently become lovers, and it felt strange to suddenly call each other by new names, so they'd fallen into the routine of calling each other "you" and themselves "me." Placeholders, perhaps, until they decided if they were going to have a future together. Or maybe that's who they were now—you and me. In which case, they definitely had a future.

Daniel stopped reading the voice-mail transcript after the first sentence. He needed to hear her voice.

He turned up the laptop's volume and clicked on the icon to play the audio file.

"Hey, you," she said, "it's me." Not angry, but her accent lacking its usual NorCal vibe. Stressed, but trying for warmth. "I know the whole world seems upside down to you right now. Bloody thing kept me in hell for six years—believe me, I understand better than anyone. But please don't duck my calls. This is important, I need to talk to you . . . face-to-face." She blew out a breath. "Don't panic, I'm not in danger or anything. But we need to meet. Soon, please. Okay, call me. Miss you. Bye."

Damn.

Daniel hadn't been ducking Kara's calls, but he had been slow-playing her, because the meditation sessions were working and he knew he was on the cusp of gaining some control over the visions. He'd decided to commit to the breakthrough, and seeing her again would be both celebration and reward for the many hours sitting zazen.

And now he couldn't see her at all. She wasn't in danger, and he wasn't about to risk that. But *Hey, babe, can't see you right now 'cause there's an assassin on my tail. Once I'm done with him, wanna go steady?* seemed a sub-optimal approach.

Daniel clicked to activate the laptop's built-in microphone.

"Hey, you," he said. "It's me. Glad you're okay and I can't wait to see you, but—" *Too casual, asshole. She's upset and you need to respect that.*

Daniel had been the one pushing for a relationship, while Kara had insisted on some time to "recombobulate" after the sudden disappearance of the voices in her head, a near-fatal stabbing (which wouldn't have happened if Daniel hadn't brought her into his world—something he thought about only a dozen times a day), and then having to remake herself with a new identity (also courtesy of her involvement with Daniel).

She'd come to visit him in Barbados before heading off on a volunteer gig for Doctors Without Borders. But on her first night there, Daniel was hit with AIT for the first time. Kara postponed her volunteer trip, stayed a month longer than she'd planned. Although Daniel's AIT hit harder than hers had, she'd been through it, so she stayed and talked him through the early stages, until he got his feet under him.

But then she left, and he didn't try to convince her to stay. She needed to figure out who she was going to be now that Kara Singh was dead, and he needed to focus on understanding his condition. She promised to visit again after her volunteer trip, and they would see where their nascent entanglement might lead.

And now she quite reasonably thought he was ducking her calls, which likely wouldn't increase his odds in the romance department.

Daniel clicked to erase the message and start over. "Hey, you. Look, you're right, we need to meet, but it's gonna have to wait, maybe . . . a week, or—"

Or what? A month?

He erased this one as well. Before he could hit Record again, his laptop speakers pinged and the transcript of a new voice-mail appeared on the screen.

This one was from Pat Wahlquist. The brief exchange above it began with the question Daniel had asked from his New York hotel room:

—Taking visitors? Need a little of your time.
—Not home. Come to Savannah and rent wheels. ETA?
—Tomorrow.

The new message read:

—Out past the Crab Shack. Paradise Marina, slip fifteen. *Miss Trixie*. Come aboard. I'll be along shortly.

Daniel closed the browser window. Kara deserved a thoughtful response, and he didn't want to risk blowing his chances by shining her on with something glib. He'd figure out what to say later.

Soon.

11

Paradise Marina proved a quiet place not far off Highway 80, near the saltwater wetlands between the mainland and Tybee Island. Two dozen boats filled the marina. Motor yachts, ocean-going sailboats, a few houseboats—none of them small, ranging perhaps between fifty and eighty feet in length.

As he walked along the jetty, Daniel could hear several WaveRunners buzzing like giant mechanical water insects in the far distance.

Docked in slip fifteen was a steel-hulled trawler with a canvas awning covering the aft deck, *Miss Trixie* painted on the stern. Daniel climbed aboard and stepped into the shade of the canvas awning. A Coleman cooler sat on the deck. Next to the cooler, a teak chair with green-and-white-striped cushions, just like the furniture on his balcony in the vision.

Weird.

Daniel put down his bag and sat in the chair, flipped the cooler's lid. Five stubby brown bottles of Red Stripe lager winked at him from their icy bath. He couldn't help but smile. *Why the hell shouldn't the universe have a sense of humor?* He rescued one of the bottles, grabbed the church key tied by a string to the cooler's handle, pried off the cap, and drank.

As promised, Pat was not aboard. He'd be out scouting, watching Daniel's arrival, making sure he hadn't grown a tail.

Daniel scanned the fully occupied marina. A mélange of live-aboard crafts owned by people with money, people who probably carried much of that money in cash. A place where it was impolite to inquire about your neighbor's background or livelihood.

If you were okay with that, it looked like a pretty nice place to drop anchor for a while. But it didn't look like the kind of place that would suit Pat's particular needs.

Pat normally lived in a brick ranch house at the end of a thin finger of land deep in the Louisiana bayou, south of Dulac. His entire property was booby-trapped. At the flip of a switch, the security system took over and the place had umpteen ways to kill you. Daniel had seen it in action, firsthand.

He had time to finish half his beer before the buzzing of a WaveRunner grew louder and Pat arrived by water, pulling alongside the slip and cutting the engine. Pat stepped onto the dock and lashed the machine securely to a cleat. He wore cutoff jean shorts and a gray hoodie emblazoned with *LSU* in big purple letters.

Daniel stood as Pat leapt aboard. "Did I come alone?"

Pat said, "Appears so." He pulled a snub-nosed revolver from the front pocket of his hoodie and put it on the table.

"Paradise must have a hell of a Neighborhood Watch."

Pat broke into a leather-faced smile, deep crow's feet framing his eyes. A couple years shy of forty, still in Navy SEAL shape, but he wore the face of a man a decade older. He said, "Good to see you not full of holes, brother," and gave Daniel a tight hug.

"Good to be not full of holes."

Pat gestured to the scenery. "Not bad, huh?" A loud crunching sound came from his right shoulder as he moved it around in a slow circle. "Doc says I gotta get it rebuilt . . . third goddamn time in ten years."

Daniel looked across the marina, to the thin line of palmettos standing like impotent sentries between the shore and the road. "Isn't this a little . . . vulnerable? What happened to constructive paranoia?"

"Was finding it less than constructive," Pat drawled, "so I gave up weed, except for my birthday. And New Year's . . . and Saint Patrick's Day, Mardi Gras, Peter Tosh's birthday, and the day Major General Smedley Butler died. Oh, and—"

Daniel held up a hand. "I get it."

"Anyway, I think we're rapidly approaching a time when mobility will be tactically superior to battlements." Pat nodded at the helm, through the cabin windows. "*Miss Trixie*'s a blue-water beauty with solar panels up top and all the tech gear. She'll save my life one of these days."

"Planning to cross the Atlantic?"

"Can if I need to. Destination TBD. I hear Barbados is nice." Pat unlocked the cabin and disappeared inside. He returned a minute later, wearing full-length jeans, a water bottle in one hand and a pack of Dunhills in the other. He sat and lit a smoke with a dented brass Zippo. "Gotta keep one vice." He snapped the lighter shut. "Raoul called last night, briefed me. They knew you'd come, of course, and they knew I'd help you if it pleased them or not. Your business is your business, so I told Raoul I won't be reporting back unless and until I think they need to be looped in, and only after arguing it out with you and either convincing you or reaching an impasse."

"Bet he loved that."

"He had a few choice words for both of us, reminded me to remind you that 'the Foundation will offer no further assistance unless and until you agree to work together moving forward,' *end quote.*"

"I'm not looking for their assistance."

"Then we good." Pat took a swig of water. "So you added another Lucien Drapeau to your fan club, client unknown. That about right?"

"That's exactly right."

Pat said, "He come at you 'cause you got AIT?"

Daniel said nothing.

Pat said, "Hey, I didn't know about it till last night, and by that time you were already on your way."

Daniel said, "What, exactly, didn't you know until last night?"

"Raoul said there was a Foundation operative named Jay Eckinsburger, a while ago, worked the AIT desk. Then one day, he came down with AIT himself. Petit mal seizures. He'd just freeze for a minute and when he snapped out of it, he'd report weird dreams about a seaside town with some huge skyscraper, and sometimes those dreams foretold future events."

Daniel swallowed some cold beer and blamed it for the chill that ran through him. "Dreams about a seaside town. With a skyscraper."

"That's what Raoul said. This Eckinsburger dude apparently went insane, became catatonic, and is currently drooling all over himself in some five-star loony bin on Long Island. But before he froze completely, he said you were coming, you had the power to save us, and you might be able to stop what he couldn't."

"Who the hell is 'us' and what couldn't he stop?"

"Story goes: dude stopped talking right after that, never specified an 'us.' As for what he was trying to stop, Raoul said that information will be available only if you come in from the cold. And he won't tell me, 'cause he knows I'd share." Pat dragged on his cigarette. "'Course, he could be bluffing. Maybe this Eckinsburger dude never said what it was he couldn't stop, before going all zombie."

Daniel thought about it. "Between us?"

"Cone of silence."

"I have AIT."

Pat sucked air through his teeth. "Coulda opened with that, you know. How long?"

"A few months. I've been studying it, keeping a journal, learning to exert at least some control over it. At its strongest, it comes on as a vision of a seaside town, so at least part of Raoul's story is probably true."

"Wait just a second. You were in that same town?"

"Yeah, I had the same vision, big skyscraper and everything."

"Damn, son." Pat sat in silence for a moment. "That is freaky. How you coping?"

Daniel hadn't spoken about his AIT with anyone since Kara's visit, and he hadn't foreseen discussing it again until her next visit. He wouldn't have come to Pat for this, not unless things became intolerable, but he was glad for it now.

"I'm coping as well as can be expected, I guess. It gets pretty weird sometimes, but knowing about AIT's existence in advance is an advantage. For starters, I don't have to wonder if I'm going insane or if I have a chemical imbalance. And having seen it up close in Tim and Kara is huge. Even though I don't know what's behind it, I can study it as some kind of natural phenomenon. A thing that happens. But none of that makes it any less weird. The visions are way beyond dreams—more conscious. And the voice, when it comes, is . . . I don't know, it's *everywhere*."

Daniel took a swig of beer. "To hell with Raoul. Ames already gave me a lead to follow." He showed Pat the thin file on Dana Cameron and explained that she was the voice in his head, the woman in his seaside vision. And he told of how the vision had provided warning, how recognizing Drapeau in the real world had given him precious seconds to make his escape.

"Okay, that's beyond freaky," said Pat. "AIT is a serious mind-fuck. I don't envy you."

"Raoul does," said Daniel. "Said he's jealous, wishes he had it."

"For such a smart guy, Raoul is sometimes an idiot," said Pat. He toasted Daniel with his water. "Respect. Seems like you're keeping your shit together like a champ."

"*Seems* being the operative word there. Truth is, sometimes I feel like I'm hanging on by my fingernails. I really need your help, Pat."

Pat dismissed it with a wave of his cigarette. "Don't be silly. You pulled my ass outta the fire when I needed it. It's what we do, brother. Hell, if you went after this guy alone, I might kill you myself just for being stupid." He dragged on his smoke. "So what's the play? We off to Barcelona?"

Daniel nodded. "Answer to your earlier question: I do think Drapeau came at me because I've got AIT." A swig of beer. "Thing is, he didn't come to fill me with holes." He shuddered at the memory. "Back of his van had a gurney with restraints and an ECT machine. He came to turn my brain to scrambled eggs."

"Well, shit. That's right nasty." Pat dragged on his smoke. "Electric lobotomy."

"That'll be the name of my punk band," said Daniel. He finished his beer and fished a new one out of the ice, and they sat in silence for a minute. He said, "Somehow, the weirdness is a little easier to accept now that the voice belongs to a real woman living in Spain. When it's just a disembodied voice coming from everywhere . . . you start to imagine that maybe it's . . . God, or the cosmic consciousness, or some other unproven thing—anything—just to define it, to solidify your reality. I mean, it's fascinating to study, but being inside of it feels a whole lot like what I imagine going crazy feels like. Be for the best if I could continue to study it without looking over my shoulder. Scrambled brains is not on my bucket list."

Pat took a deep drag on his cigarette, blew out the smoke, and dropped the butt into one of the empty bottles.

"We'll get this guy," he said. "I promise."

12

Universitat de Barcelona—Spain

The brass nameplate mounted on the old oak door read:

DR. DANA CAMERON.

Daniel knocked three times.

Her voice came, not from everywhere at once, not from within his head, but simply from behind the door. "Come."

Daniel turned the knob, stepped inside the wood-paneled office, and closed the door. Cameron sat at a carved desk, flipping through a stack of printed pages, an uncapped green highlighter in her hand. She wore the same purple glasses that she had worn in Daniel's vision, and under a tweed blazer she wore the same black T-shirt with *Wake Up!* in white brushstroke across the chest. At the edge of the desk was a hardcover book: *The Truth (So Far) about Trinity*, by Julia Rothman.

"Gimme a minute," she said, without looking up. "Grab a chair."

Daniel sat in a visitor's chair, fighting to collect his thoughts. This was not like seeing Drapeau in Barbados after seeing him in a premonitory vision. Tim had seen Angelica Ory in a vision and Kara had seen the victims in Liberia, so Daniel had been prepared for that. But he'd never imagined that the all-encompassing voice living in his head, loosening his grip on reality, belonged to an actual person—and that this actual person would one day be sitting across from him. Seeing her photo had been a shock, but hearing her voice, sitting face-to-face . . .

She flipped another two pages, stopped, and dragged the highlighter across a few lines of text near the bottom of the page.

Then she did look up. The highlighter dropped from her hand and clattered on the desktop.

"Crap," she said. "What are you doing here? When I said come find me, I meant to cross—" She stopped abruptly, pushed her glasses up her nose. "Wait. How *did* you find me?"

Daniel tried twice before getting the words out. "Excuse me, I'm . . . I'm processing a slight shift in reality and it's causing some cognitive dissonance, and I'm trying—" He caught himself mid-ramble, stopped. "But you don't seem—"

"I've been navigating both sides for a while," she said. "Not my first time. Yes, I have been in your head, and yes, I'm real. Take that as given, and explain how you found me here."

He said, "I couldn't even tell you. I mean, why do I even have your voice in my head? Why are you wearing clothes I saw in a vision? I haven't had this condition very long and I'm still trying to get my bearings. You said you could help me."

Cameron's expression hardened. "Get the hell out of my office." She nodded at the door. "Go on, take a hike."

"Wait, what?"

"I saved your life. You think I'm risking my neck so you can walk in here and lie to my face? I don't need this."

She was right. If she hadn't brought Daniel out of the vision when she did, he'd still have been meditating when Drapeau arrived at his cottage. She really had saved his life.

He held up his hands. "I'm sorry, you're right. That was just a reflex. Trust has been in short supply lately. I apologize. How I found you: Lucien Drapeau came for me at home—"

"Who?"

"The man in the yellow suit, the man you saved me from." Daniel thought back to the file Ames had given him. "You might know him as Larry Elias?"

"Just Elias." She nodded. "Go on."

"He came for me at home, and a security camera picked up his face. I know some people who have the ability to tap into the surveillance web, and they found him on the University of Barcelona's security footage, signing in under the name Larry Elias. Signing in to see you. So the people I know pulled your driver's license, and I recognized your photo. That's the truth, that's how I found you."

Cameron nodded. "Okay, better. And now you're looking for him?"

"He tried to kill me. Yes, I'm looking for him."

"Good. But you shouldn't have come here. If he followed you, if he sees us together—"

"He didn't, and he won't. I've got a man stationed outside, watching our backs. A security pro. The phone in my pocket will vibrate if we need to move."

"Put the phone on the desk where I can see it."

Daniel did. Cameron rolled her chair to the credenza, poured bourbon into a couple of rocks glasses, and rolled back. He took the offered glass with a nod of thanks.

"In the vision you said *Noah's* soldiers were all around, and Drapeau also said the name. Who is he, and why are you afraid of him?"

Cameron gazed into her bourbon for a moment. Then she took a sip. "Doesn't work that way, kiddo. I told you to cross over, but no, you had to put me at risk coming here instead. So you get to go first. Talk."

But where to begin? Daniel looked to the credenza, eyeing the little metal racehorse atop the bottle's cork. "Blanton's was my uncle's go-to whiskey, as well." He nodded to Julia's book. "Tim Trinity was my uncle." Cameron's eyebrows rose, but she said nothing. Daniel said, "I didn't have AIT until three months ago, but I was Julia's original unnamed source, the one who brought Trinity's condition to her attention when she was at the *Times-Picayune*. After Tim died, I joined . . . a very well-funded, covert investigation into AIT."

She leaned forward and rested her elbows on the desk. "What did you learn that's not in the book?"

"A lot. We know the phenomenon, whatever it is, waxes and wanes throughout history, like ribbons moving closer together and farther apart, sometimes going almost completely dormant for hundreds of years at a time. We know it reawakens during periods of disruptive change in the course of human affairs—the collapse and rise of empires, for example, or rapid depopulations by disease or world war. And we know AIT is on the march again, easily over one hundred thousand cases and spreading faster by the month."

"That's all you know?"

"Wish it were. There are groups of powerful people who know about AIT and are trying to harness it, control it, because they think the information it provides would give them ultimate control over the power structures of the world."

Cameron waved her hand. "They don't matter."

"Uh, I think they do matter," said Daniel. "I've seen what they're capable of. They wiped out an entire village in Liberia. They were behind the terror attack in South Carolina. They've bioengineered a plague bacterium that causes AIT in two percent of its victims. There's a truce in place keeping it on ice for now, but—"

"Daniel, they don't matter. They haven't got a clue about what's really happening. What else?"

Daniel sipped his drink. "I met a couple of other people with AIT, before I got it. Like Tim, they had voices in their heads and they had visions. But their visions didn't include the seaside town, and neither did my uncle's. But you and I have the seaside town vision, and I've heard of another man named Jay Eckinsburger who had it before he went insane and became uncommunicative."

Cameron shook her head. "They're two different things, Daniel. AIT is a mere shadow of what we have. AIT is a few grains of salt spilling from a shaker, while we're drinking straight from the ocean. A tiny percentage of people with AIT cross over. More every day, but there are only a couple thousand of us. Everyone else is dreaming."

"No offense intended," said Daniel, "but that sounds a bit crazy."

"It gets much crazier, I promise." She sipped her drink. "This is why I told you to cross over. Words are . . . limiting. I need to *show* it to you." With some edge, she added, "Which I'd have already done if you hadn't resisted the last time I called you."

"Forgive me, Dr. Cameron, I do appreciate you saving my life— maybe I should've opened with that. But cut me a little slack. Living with your voice in my head, seeing you in a vision, and now seeing you here . . . actually, I don't have a word for how deeply weird it is."

Cameron conceded the point with a nod. "Fair enough. But follow my lead next time, and come for the guided tour, okay?" She held her glass forward.

Daniel clicked his against it. "Deal," he said, and they drank to it. After a moment, he said, "Drapeau's a high-end freelance assassin, with probably hundreds of clients. This Noah you're afraid of, you think he could be the one who wants me dead?"

"If he didn't want you dead, Elias wouldn't be after you. In fact, you're the reason Elias came to see me here."

"What did he say?"

"Just reminded me that I'm not to interact with you. Then went through his talking points about the need for structure and cohesion, and I nodded and assured him I understood. He didn't have to threaten me—I already know they'll stop at nothing."

"He'd warned you about me before?"

"First time was about three months ago. Elias—Drapeau, to you—said you were coming, and not to have contact with you. They'd never warned me off a specific arrival before. I figured if they were worried about you, it was a good enough reason to help, so I tried to reach out to you. All I had to focus on was your name. You're a little younger than I imagined, but otherwise my mental picture of you was pretty close."

"But you don't have any idea why Noah's taken an interest in—?"

"I don't have all the answers. You've got voices and visions? Guess what, so do I. And ever since I reached out to you, I've had this recurring dream—a premonition of a devastated city—"

"—with a thousand people dead, you told me."

"And you're standing in the middle of it, and you feel . . ." She held his gaze, unblinking. "You feel awful, because you caused it to happen."

A chill ran through Daniel. He wanted to insist that he would never do such a thing, but he was all too familiar with the law of unintended consequences. "What city?"

She shook her head. "I didn't recognize any landmarks. But unless something changes, I think it's going to happen."

"So who the hell is Noah?"

"I don't even know *what* he is, ultimately, much less *who*. But he basically runs the place. And he's not Elias's client, more like . . ." She sipped her drink and thought for a moment. "You said Drapeau's a freelance assassin. He may be, but that's not the real him. Elias is the real him, and he's no freelancer. He's only got one mission in life."

"And that is?"

"To please his master."

"Then let's talk about his master."

"Don't get ahead of yourself, Daniel. We need to take this a step at a time."

"Okay, but you said Noah runs the place. I don't understand that. How does someone run a vision in my head, or shared meditative visualization, or whatever the hell this is?"

"See, that's exactly what I mean—we have to get you situated first. It isn't a vision. You have to stop thinking of it that way. It's a place. You'll just have to come with me and experience it for yourself to understand."

"A *place*?" said Daniel. "A place where dumpsters appear out of nowhere. A place where the sun doesn't move in the sky. Where license plates and newspapers glow so bright you can't look at them?"

"Yes. But still a place. You're thinking of it as a dream, as something that exists in your mind, when it's the other way around. Your mind exists in it."

A place with a frozen sun, where some things just appear and other things glow when you look at them.

Daniel shook his head. "When you said it gets crazier, you were not lying."

"A lot to wrap your head around. If you chase the metaphysics of it too hard, it'll drive you mad. And that's not a figure of speech. I've seen it happen."

"People have been tying themselves in knots over the nature of reality since Plato," said Daniel.

"Still, in order to navigate it without freaking out completely, you need a mental construct for it. A way to plug the experiential evidence into your reality tunnel. We all do. I can't predict what metaphor will work for you, all I can offer you is a look through *my* reality tunnel."

13

"Pull up over here." Dana Cameron pointed and Pat guided the rental across two lanes and stopped at the curb.

Daniel followed Cameron's gaze to the storefront on their right. The sign in the window read:

LA TERAPIA DE FLOTACIÓN.

"Wait a second," he said. "Sensory deprivation?"

Cameron said, "That's the old term. Now it's called *float therapy*."

"Changing the name doesn't change what it is."

"Don't worry, it's fun. Anyway, it's the fastest way to get where we need to go."

Daniel looked at Pat.

Pat shrugged. "I hear it's the new yoga."

Cameron checked them into the luxury float spa and bought Daniel swim trunks. The young man at the counter wore a skintight FC Barcelona jersey and his hair tied up in a man-bun. In another life, he might've been a fashion model.

Cameron handed Daniel the trunks, dug into her briefcase, and pulled out a red one-piece. "Let's take room three," she said. "It's a double."

✠ ✠ ✠

The swim trunks were a little loose at the waist and didn't have a string, so in the interest of modesty, Daniel kept a thumb hooked in the waistband. The twin fiberglass float tanks were white and windowless, with a hatch door at the foot end. They looked like twin cocoons.

Or caskets.

Cameron had paid cash at the front desk, no plastic. No one knew Daniel was here. They'd left her cell phone back in her office. If Lucien Drapeau happened to be in town and decided to track her down, the phone would lead him to the university. Still . . .

As if reading Daniel's mind, Pat said, "I'll be standing watch." He clasped Daniel on the shoulder. "Got your six."

Cameron entered from the changing room, wearing the red one-piece. At the center of her chest was the Flash's lightning-bolt logo.

She said, "Inside the tank is water so salty you float on top, can't sink. Even unconscious, you just lie on your back and float. The water and air inside are both set for body temperature. And of course there's no light at all, not a single photon. After a few minutes, you can't even feel your body." She smiled at the thought. "You become just a mind, floating in space. It's really cool."

"What if I have one of those adrenaline rushes in there?"

"There's a big red button on the inside wall, opens the door. But you won't. The adrenaline rush only happens when part of your mind doesn't want to go, or doesn't want to come back. Indecision, or outright resistance, will trigger a rush, but if you go and return intentionally, you get a smooth ride, no jet lag. Just quiet your mind, feel your body fade, and then decide to go. It's really that simple."

"Okay. Then what happens?"

"You'll wake up standing on the beach where you saw me before. I'll be there with you. I'll look just like I did last time. Expect to see me, and you will. Remember, everything runs on intention and attention." Daniel started to speak but she cut him off, gesturing to the float tank on the right. "I'll explain there, just get in."

Pat opened the hatch. "Your chariot awaits."

Daniel climbed into the tank. The chamber was about seven feet long, four feet wide, and tall enough to sit up in, but just. The warm water came up to his ribs, and the equally warm air smelled clean and slightly salty. There was a blue LED strip set into the ceiling just above Daniel's head, and the water glowed blue.

Daniel gave Pat a thumbs-up and Pat closed the hatch, and he was alone in his blue cocoon. Next to the hatch there was the red button and a light switch. Daniel flipped the switch, plunging himself into absolute blackness.

He lay on his back, weightless. After a few minutes, he could no longer feel any line of demarcation between his skin and the air and water surrounding him. He could almost feel the boundary of what was *him* and what was *not him* melting away, until there was none. There was no meaningful difference between up and down, no difference between eyes open and closed.

Daniel didn't feel *deprived* of sensory input, but freed from its constant nattering. Free of gravity, free of sight. And in this freedom, he pictured himself standing on the beach of that seaside town. He visualized Dana Cameron standing before him until he expected to see her there.

"Open your eyes."

14

Daniel let out the breath he was holding and filled his lungs again. He was standing barefoot on the beach, the seaside town to his right, sun hanging in the western sky over the ocean to his left. Dana Cameron stood facing him. Purple glasses, red T-shirt, blue beach wrap.

Just like last time.

She pointed at his feet. "Wiggle your toes."

"What?"

"For a soft landing, you want to focus on a specific sensory stimulus as soon as you arrive. Feel the sand between your toes."

Daniel wiggled his toes, feeling both the grit and warmth of the sand.

"Feels real, doesn't it?"

"Yes, it does. But I know my body's in a float tank in Barcelona right now."

Cameron shook her head. "This is your body, right here."

Daniel pinched the skin of his forearm. Felt real, but the notion was simply impossible. "I don't—then what's in the float tank in Barcelona?"

"Your secondary body, at best. Probably not even that."

"Wait, no, no, no . . . It's one thing to say this is a real place, but you expect me to believe *this place* supersedes what I, perhaps quaintly, call *real life*? Because—"

Cameron clapped her hands together. "Stop talking. Just stop." She shook her head. "God, *men.* Now shut up and let me lead, or this isn't gonna work."

"Fine," said Daniel, forcing a long breath. "Mea culpa."

She pointed at his feet again. "Feel the sand with your feet. Don't think. Just observe. Put your *attention* on it."

Daniel made arches with his feet, fists with his toes, feeling the texture of the sand as it came into detail, then sharper still—impossibly sharp—until he could feel each individual grain of sand, distinct from the others. A hyper-detailed version of sand.

"Incredible," he said. "I can almost count them."

"Never has there been sand so real," Cameron said with a smile. "Now. Move through your body and observe what your senses are telling you."

Daniel wrestled his attention from the sand under his feet to the warm breeze caressing his face and arms and hands. He found he could track the path of the air as it pushed its way through the hair on his forearms. The breeze smelled like the ocean, and while the float tank could've provided the salt, there was also a subtle vegetal smell. Seaweed perhaps, or the nearby aloe plants. In addition to the sound of the wind, Daniel heard every detail of the sea lapping on the beach, hissing into the sand and rolling back out.

He watched Dana Cameron's hair dance in the breeze, then turned his gaze to the sloped street rising into town. The same houses and low-rise, white stucco apartments with terra-cotta roofs, and cars parked at the curb here and there. Far in the distance, the gleaming white tower rose into the sky, to a height never seen in what Daniel still wanted to think of as *real life*.

A thought returned to him. A thought he'd had on a previous visit, shortly after leaving the apartment up the hill. But now it had context.

This moment—in this place—feels more real than any moment I've ever experienced in that other place.

Not a dream, not a vision, not any creation of Daniel's mind. It was a place, as real—maybe more real—than the place from which he'd come.

Daniel tried the thought out several times, wording it in different ways. But however he put it, he couldn't make it sound like a lie. He turned back to face Dana Cameron, realized his mouth was open, and closed it.

She spread her arms out to her sides. "And the scales fell from the eyes of the blind man."

✚ ✚ ✚

They walked side by side along the beach, ocean on their left and town to the right, Daniel soaking in the sights, sounds, smells—all the physical sensations. There was no dodging it—this was some sort of reality. Strange compared with the one he'd known all his life, but an actual place, strangeness notwithstanding.

"Okay, Dr. Cameron," said Daniel, "hit me with your reality tunnel. How the hell do you make sense of this place?"

Cameron said, "Are you familiar with the idea of the holographic universe?"

Daniel nodded. He'd spent a decade working as a Vatican investigator, testing and debunking miracle claims. Until Tim Trinity, he'd never found one that made the grade, but he'd come across a few anomalies that resisted conventional explanation, and he'd read up on quantum mechanics in search of answers, finding only more questions.

He said, "In physics, the holographic principle says the universe we experience in 3-D is actually just a hologram."

"Some would say a consciousness hologram." She waved that away. "But I'm getting ahead of myself. Thanks to quantum physics, we know the universe is virtually non-material. The solidity of matter is an illusion."

"Not if you fall down the stairs and crack your head," said Daniel.

"Don't be a smartass. If even one subatomic particle of your body made contact with one particle of the stairs, you'd explode. You don't crack your head on the stairs; you crack the idea of your head on the idea of the stairs. Because you never actually *touch* anything. Not falling down, not making love. There is no actual contact between things. Things, including our bodies, are made almost entirely of nothingness."

"Okay," said Daniel, "but people have been saying *reality is an illusion* since long before Plato. How does this help us?"

"I warned you about chasing the metaphysics too hard. Back in the so-called 'real world,' we don't have any idea what *consciousness* is, metaphysically, much less what reality is. It's the reality we've known since birth, so most of us can be reasonably comfortable in it as long as we *pretend* we know these things. But through science and mathematics and technology, we developed the ability to measure beyond our physical senses, and one thing we know for sure: The universe is fundamentally *different* than what our senses tell us. You want to know the mind of God? Or if there even is one? Ultimate reality? You're shit out of luck. Coming here doesn't give you that."

✤ ✤ ✤

Daniel sat on the beach, marveling at the ocean's surface as it rippled and glittered beneath the sun. He sifted handfuls of sand through his fingers, enjoying its intensely detailed texture. He couldn't avoid the sense that he was feeling sand—real sand—for the very first time.

Absurd.

Cameron found a stick under a nearby tree, brought it back, and stood at Daniel's feet. "For our purposes, the holographic metaphor works like this." She used the stick to draw a large circle in the sand. "This is the known universe." She began stabbing the sand inside the circle, making dozens of little depressions. "Now imagine this entire circle covered in dots—hundreds of billions of them—and each is a galaxy. Some of the larger dots are superclusters—tens of millions of galaxies grouped together into massive structures. And each galaxy has maybe a hundred billion stars, with God knows how many planets, moons, asteroids, comets. And we keep on zooming in closer, until we're standing on Earth, looking up at the sky. We have no idea what the hell all this is, but we look up at countless points of light and we know there's a lot of *stuff* in the universe. Another thing our senses tell us is that this *stuff* is solid. We know because we fall down and crack our heads. But that's not reality. Our senses lie. Really, all the stuff in the universe isn't stuff at all. It's all just a swirling dance of energy and information. Physically, that's virtually all there is, but when we observe it, it presents itself in a way that appears to us as a universe made of solid, material stuff."

She drew a happy face outside the large circle. "Some people think there's a god who thought the physical universe into existence and then put us here to experience it. Some say we're just a dream God is having."

She scratched out God's happy face and drew a big happy face in the big circle. "Others think the very universe, this dance of energy and information, is itself a living consciousness, that we're like nerve endings of a sentient universe, a way for the universe to observe itself." She used the stick to scratch out the universe. "Of course these are only metaphors, to reassure us about what we don't know. The truth, if we ever learn it, will be none of those things. It'll probably be something we've not even imagined." Her expression darkened as she tossed the stick aside. "Meanwhile, humans seem incapable of accepting metaphysical uncertainty, and we're perfectly willing to kill each other over whose metaphor is 'real.'"

Cameron sat on the beach beside Daniel and looked out to sea. She let out a dry laugh. "At first we were like explorers, those of us who crossed over. We'd just discovered a new land—only it was a new reality. We'd gather together at the end of the day and share our experiences, teach each other what we'd learned. And we'd discuss and debate the big, unanswerable *What's it all about, Alfie?* questions. None of us were dead on Earth, so it stood to reason this wasn't any kind of afterlife—more like a parallel life. But what kind of parallel life, and how did it relate to the reality we came here from and returned to? Asking the big questions was both frightening and exciting, and it became the official party game around here. The one thing we all agreed on was that none of us knew the answers. We used to welcome newcomers with parties on the beach. They'd go all night long sometimes. Music, dancing, champagne. It was beautiful, then."

"How long ago was this?"

"Time doesn't really mean the same thing here, but the first time I crossed over completely was almost nine months ago, in Earth time. There were a few hundred already here when I arrived."

"*Earth* time?"

"At first, we just called the place we came from 'back home.' Earth became the more formal term. Not to suggest we're on another planet—we had no idea where we were, we just knew we weren't in Kansas anymore. Many of us suspected that our consciousnesses—our awareness—had crossed over into a parallel universe with slightly different physical rules. You know, maybe we'd popped into the universe next door, our minds now in a collapsed-dimension universe, in the dark energy/dark matter universe, or whatever. But as we learned more about how this place works, we realized this place is *fundamental* to that place, if you will. So the holographic metaphor became our working hypothesis. The place we came from—the universe that contains Earth—is a hologram. And this place is like the universal hologram projector. So we named this place Source. We still call the other place Earth, but very few still call it home."

Daniel said, "Given that humans like to believe they're at the center of everything—"

"Yes, I know. But we don't call this Source because of our ego. We call it Source because that metaphor fits the evidence. It's not just that our senses pick up more detail here. Here, we're like minor gods. We can manipulate reality." She shifted her position to sit cross-legged, facing Daniel. "Do like this," she said, and Daniel mirrored her. "Now look behind you."

Daniel twisted his torso and looked down the beach. "What am I—"

"Okay, turn back."

He did. Cameron sat as before, but the red Flash T-shirt was gone, replaced by the black *Wake Up!* T-shirt.

He heard himself laugh. "That was incredibly cool."

"I know, right? And it's easy, too. I'll show you how to do it. Close your eyes."

Daniel did.

"Open them."

Cameron hadn't changed, but a hand-carved wooden box now sat between them on the sand.

"Look in the box."

Daniel opened the hinged lid and looked inside.

"It's empty."

"Close the lid. Good. Now I want you to name something you saw in my office or at the float spa, something I would be familiar with and that could fit in the box." She closed her eyes.

Daniel said, "Your highlighter, the one you were using when I came to your office."

After a moment, she opened her eyes and gave Daniel a cocky grin. "Open the box."

He flipped the lid and reached in, pulled out the green highlighter. He turned it over in his hands, pulled the cap off, and dragged a green line on the back of his hand.

"Schrödinger's highlighter," he said. "Amazing. So Drapeau really did manifest dumpsters into existence."

"He's very powerful," said Cameron. "I don't think I could do dumpsters, no matter how long I practiced." She reached forward and closed the lid on the empty box. "FYI, Drapeau goes by Elias here. No one in Source knows him as Drapeau."

Daniel said, "What do they call you in Source?"

"They call me Digger."

"Seriously?"

She laughed. "As I said, we were like explorers. I'm an archeologist, so I manifested a trowel and started digging. The name began as a joke, but I liked it, so it stuck." The breeze blew and she brushed some hair from her face. "Call me Digger, at least while we're here. We'll come up with a Source name for you later."

Daniel caught some movement in the corner of his eye, but it was just a tree branch swaying slightly in the breeze. He said, "Are we safe? Is there some possibility that Drap—Elias, whatever—could just show up and start hurling heavy things at us?"

She shook her head. "I'd feel his presence nearby. It's a thing you can do here. Now look at the box. You're about to make magic. I want you to think of an object without telling me, something that you know intimately, something I've never seen, that would fit in the box. Nod when you've got it."

"Do I close my eyes?"

"I do, but not everyone does. Stare unfocused at the box, or close your eyes. Whatever feels comfortable."

Daniel stared at the box, focusing past it. He thought of his uncle's switchblade, picturing the horn scales, chipped at the edge of the steel safety catch, bringing the knife into sharp focus. He nodded.

"Now put your attention inside the box, and visualize the object in the box. See it in the box, expect it to be there, and open the box."

Daniel opened the box.

Empty.

She said, "That's because you didn't really expect it to be there. You wanted it to be there, but that's not enough." She reached forward and closed the lid. "I've done it hundreds of times, so don't try to match my speed. To manipulate reality, you have to believe in the new reality you're trying to manifest. You have to *know* it's going to be there before you open the box."

Daniel stared at the box again, unfocused his eyes, visualized the switchblade inside the box. He took a couple of long decompression breaths, and he felt the subtle shift. He was no longer visualizing the knife; he was seeing it. It was in the box. He knew it like he knew his name.

He lifted the lid, reached inside, curled his fingers around the familiar shape, and pulled the switchblade out of the box. He pressed the button, and the steel blade snapped to attention. He turned the knife and read the words he knew by heart, stamped at the base of the blade:

ROMANELLI
Import & Export Co.
ITALY

He held the knife in his right hand, gently pricked the index finger of his left with the blade's sharp tip. He watched as a drop of blood rose, round and red, glistening in the sun. He dragged his finger against his tongue, and the coppery taste flooded his mouth. Like the Platonic form of the taste of blood.

Then came a crazy urge. He said, "If I slashed my own throat right now, would I wake up in Barcelona?"

Her eyes widened and she held up a hand. "No," she said. "If you die here, you die. Same as back home. You think I saved your life because you had a warning when Elias came for you at your house, but I actually saved it here, in the alley. Don't be casual about this place, Daniel, or you won't live long."

15

Remember when you said AIT waxes and wanes like ribbons moving closer together and farther apart?" said Digger as they walked up the road. "Think of Earth and Source as the ribbons, like membrane universes. When they get close, AIT spreads. If they get close enough, people start crossing over."

"What if they touch?"

"If Source is fundamental, then if the ribbons touch, the universe containing Earth would . . . pop like a soap bubble. It would simply cease to exist."

She stopped walking and looked up at the apartment building to their left. Then she turned to face Daniel, the building behind her.

"Okay, lesson number two might blow your mind a little," she said. "You thought the box was fun, wait'll you see this. Close your eyes for a few seconds. Then open them."

Daniel closed his eyes, counted three slow Mississippis, and opened them again.

She was thirty feet away, waving down at him from a second-floor balcony.

"No way," he said.

"Way," she called back.

He walked toward her. "You just freaking *teleported* yourself."

"It's something we can do here in Source. Cool, huh? We call it spot-traveling."

Daniel stepped onto the sidewalk directly below her. "Teach me," he said.

Digger shook her head. "I'll talk you through the steps, but it's not like the highlighter trick. Took me twenty-three tries before I could even spot-travel a yard." She leaned her elbows on the balcony wall. "You start with a few slow breaths, while looking at the space you want to occupy. You put your attention on that spot, knowing that if you can *see* a place, you can *be* there. Then you close your eyes, visualize yourself in the new space, and expect to be there when you open them again."

"That's it?"

"That's it. But it's harder than it sounds, so don't get frustrated. Pick a spot about a foot in front of you." She turned her back. "Whenever you're ready."

Daniel started to focus on the space directly in front of him, but then, on sheer impulse, he shifted his gaze up to the space beside Dana Cameron—*Digger here*—on the balcony. He took a couple of decompression breaths, putting his attention on that space. *If you can see a place, you can be there.* He closed his eyes, pictured himself standing beside her, expecting to open them again up on the balcony.

He opened his eyes.

On the balcony.

Facing Digger.

She jumped at the sight of him. "Oh my god," she said. "I can't believe you just did that."

His heart pounded and his head started spinning and she went out of focus.

She reached forward and grabbed his forearm. "Breathe."

He gasped out the breath he was holding and filled his lungs again, bracing his free hand on the balcony wall. Two more deep breaths, and the world stopped moving and she came back into focus.

"Okay," he said, straightening. "I'm all right."

She let go of his arm. "Pro tip: Breathing is important."

"Thanks, Coach," he said. Another deep breath brought him back to normal. "Aside from the forgetting-to-breathe part, it was easier than you said."

"You've got mad skills, kiddo; don't sell yourself short. I've never seen anything like that on the first attempt . . . or the hundredth, for that matter."

Daniel said, "In order for me to spot-travel, you turned your back. Same thing with the box and the T-shirt, right? You can't manifest something while someone's looking. Elias manifested the dumpsters behind me. When I spun around, he did the same with the gate. I never actually saw them come into existence."

She nodded. "Remember I said everything runs on intention and attention? I think of it like collapsing a probability wave by observation—by putting your attention on it. So, when you observe something, the 'wavicle' is a particle, but when you look away it's freed to become a wave function, malleable by intention, until it's observed again."

"Wow," said Daniel. "That's pretty *out there*."

She laughed. "Just a metaphor that helps me keep my reality tunnel from shattering so completely I lose my mind. Of course, I have no idea how it *actually* works."

Daniel leaned his forearms on the balcony wall, questions tumbling over each other in his mind. This was, indeed, a lot to wrap his head around.

Over his shoulder, Digger said, "I'm gonna get a beer, you want one?"

Daniel turned to face her. "How do you know—wait, you just put the beer in the fridge, didn't you?"

She smiled and tapped a finger against her temple. "Minor gods," she said. "You try it. Pick a beer you know, close your eyes, see it in the fridge." As she went inside, she called back, "Go."

Daniel closed his eyes and visualized a six-pack of Dragon Stout inside a closed refrigerator. It seemed to happen very fast, the switch from *visualizing* to *seeing*. So fast he doubted himself, didn't open his eyes yet. He began again, but was interrupted by the feeling of a cold bottle being pressed into his hand. He opened his eyes. He was holding a bottle of Dragon Stout.

"Cheers," she said, clinking a Sam Adams against the bottle in his hand.

Daniel laughed and took a long swallow of the stout. He felt the viscous texture of the brew as it coated his tongue and the roof of his mouth, slid down his throat. The taste sensation that came along with it was indescribably rich.

Like tasting the real thing for the very first time.

"I love it here," he said.

Her smile fell as she turned slightly away, leaning on the wall beside him and looking down at the sea.

"So did I," she said.

"You said you used to have beach parties that went all night long. But . . ." Daniel gestured to the sun, still hanging in the same spot above the sea. He felt a hint of vertigo and wondered if he would ever get used to a world where it was always *magic hour*.

"It used to move," she said. "Stopped just before . . . No one knows why."

"Before Noah arrived," Daniel nudged.

She almost winced at the name. Each time Daniel had asked about Noah in her office, she'd steered the conversation elsewhere, and she'd avoided saying Noah's name. She'd tried to disguise it in her office, but here it was unavoidable. The topic of Noah clearly made her apprehensive. More than.

"I need to know about him, Digger. I know I promised to let you lead—"

"So let me," she said. "I have to do this my way." She took a deep breath, refocusing. "It was about five months ago, in Earth time, when everything changed. After the sun stopped, it was even harder to judge time here, because you don't have to eat or sleep in Source unless you want to. Without physiological cues like hunger or fatigue, you come to rely on the celestial changes to track time. After all, you can't go around counting breaths or Mississippis all day."

"Why not manifest a wristwatch, same as a switchblade or a highlighter?"

"We tried that, even before the sun stopped," said Digger. "Problem is, looking at a watch is just like the license plates and newspapers and street signs and a dozen other things. It just glims out."

"Glims."

She nodded. "We call it the *glimmer*—or the *glim*. Nobody understands it, either. My own way of looking at it is: Our previous reality on Earth can be described as a *disguised* hologram—the universe doesn't appear to our senses as a hologram, but like we were saying before, when we measure down to the quantum realm, we see that what appears material is mostly non-material. Yes?"

"Yes."

"Good. But in Source, the universe appears to our senses as non-material, at least to the extent that we can manipulate reality by manifesting things into existence and manifesting ourselves in different locations. Yes?"

"I'm following you," said Daniel. "As crazy as it sounds."

"Good. So our brains—minds, whatever—perceive a truer version of reality here, and maybe they also don't lie to us here. Newspapers, street signs, license plates—those details would establish Source as a specific place in the universe we're familiar with, just as reading the time on a watch would tell us that this place works on conventional time. But here, our minds won't fill in those details, because that would be false. We interpret this place as a seaside town, but really, we're just swimming in the sea of energy and information. The metaphors we take as truth to calm ourselves back on Earth insist on remaining metaphors in Source. This whole place may be just a consciousness hologram—I mean, why even have street signs and license plates and newspaper boxes at all, right?"

Daniel smiled. "Our minds expect them to exist, so they do. But if we try to examine them, we're asking the universe to lie to us."

"And here, that makes us feel queasy," she said.

Even as a metaphor, it was beyond weird. But once again, weirdness notwithstanding, Daniel had to admit it felt . . . true.

Digger said, "You're wondering if I've dropped a lot of acid in my life. The answer is no, never."

Daniel laughed. "Not what I was thinking, I promise. When I lived in Barbados, I took up surfing. After some practice I could ride okay, but I couldn't really *carve* the waves like I wanted to. My neighbor up the gap was a Rastaman named Natty B, the town's root doctor. Natty B was a regular at the Soup Bowl, and I tell you, the man could surf. He made it look so easy, and I wanted to surf with that kind of grace. He sat me down one day, told me the secret I was missing. He said, 'You'll never achieve union with the wave while thinking about the properties of hydrodynamics.' It was a revelation, and it changed me from a guy on a surfboard into a surfer."

"It's beautiful," said Digger. "*Union with the wave*—I love it. That's very much like how this place was, before Noah. We didn't get too caught up with trying to define our experience here. We stayed focused on learning to *do stuff*, how to surf the wave. I know I make us sound like some kind of hippie commune, but it wasn't all beach parties. The freedom was exhilarating, but also frightening, and some found it more terrifying than they could bear.

"In the months before the sun stopped, the population quadrupled, multiple newcomers every day. But over a hundred people took their own lives during that same span, and maybe two hundred more simply lost their minds. Drove themselves mad, trying to discover what this place *is*, instead of learning how to exist here. Ridiculous, since we don't even know what the universe we came from *is*."

She allowed herself to ride a memory for a few moments, then came back. "And one afternoon, the sun stopped." She turned and pointed to the white tower in the east. "And soon a small glimmer appeared on the eastern horizon. The glimmer started to rise, the tower manifesting beneath it, floor by floor. If you stared at it long enough, you could see it rising, it happened so fast." She took a swig of beer. "We were all transfixed. This building was breaking the rules, appearing *while we were looking at it*, clearly being manifested by an intelligence of far greater power than us.

"Three of our best spot-travelers volunteered to go on a reconnaissance mission, check it out. They could jump a few blocks at a time, so we expected them back by the time the tower grew another dozen floors, but they didn't return and the building just kept rising, the glim like a penthouse floor on top. It got so tall you could see it from the beach at the bottom of the hill.

"The beach was our usual meeting place, so we all gravitated there to watch it together. When the tower got to the height you see now, it just stopped. And a glimmer then appeared right among us on the beach—the air shimmered and brightened until I had to shield my eyes—and it disappeared just as fast. And . . . *he* stood in its place. He glimmed into existence right in front of our eyes."

"Nice trick," said Daniel.

"No doubt. People fell to their knees."

"They thought he was God." Daniel was careful not to use Noah's name.

"Many did. And many more came to believe over time. Almost everyone. They abandoned the town, and they all live in that tower like it's some kind of holy temple. They come out to greet newcomers, and they still try to recruit the stragglers. They've recruited most of us, there may be two hundred Independents left, maybe fewer. We have to keep our heads down these days. We can't exactly gather for a head count."

"What happens when you gather?" said Daniel.

"I'm getting to it. Anyway, they try to recruit us—they assure us they're free to come and go as they please but insist that they've found the truth, and they invite us to come see for ourselves. It's like a cult, I'm telling you. Every time they come out for the newcomers, they also try to recruit the remaining stragglers. And they don't really let us greet the newcomers anymore. They always show up and butt in."

"Sure," said Daniel. "He wants his perspective to be the first impression, so he sends the true believers out to start selling the con."

She said, "But in your case, it was different. Elias was sent out ahead of time to tell the Independents you were coming and to remind us that they run the intake program. That's actually what Elias called it—the intake program. We used to just call it a welcome party on the beach." She jutted her chin at the top of the tower. "*He* has ruined everything beautiful here." Turning back to Daniel, she said, "That's enough about him for now."

"Digger, I can't help you unless I know what you know."

"I didn't ask for your help," she said. "I reached out to help you. I'm trying to stop you from destroying a city."

Daniel shook his head. "You said it yourself: They're worried about me. As powerful as he is, they're worried about me." He sipped his stout. "Remember I told you there was a man named Jay Eckinsburger who'd been to Source? He told some people I was coming with enough power to stop something. To 'save us' he said. I don't know if 'us' meant the people here, and I don't know what that something is, but I have a pretty strong inkling it lives up in that tower. And you're holding back information—you know far more than you're saying."

Digger held his gaze. "If I told you everything you know now—not just that Source is a real place, but everything about manifesting and spot-traveling—if I told you all that when we first met, would you have believed me?"

"No, of course not."

"So you'll just have to trust me to pace it."

Daniel swallowed some beer as an ugly thought descended.

He said, "Working his faith-healer act on the tent-revival circuit, my uncle always proclaimed himself *one of God's chosen messengers.* And I believed it as a kid. Many years later, when he was struck with AIT and learned—along with the rest of the world—that he was predicting the future, he came to believe that his lie had become truth. That God had now chosen him to deliver a message to the world. He even foresaw his own death, and he still chose not to wear that damn vest. I wish he'd worn it."

He turned the cool bottle in his hands, grounding himself. "My uncle, having no way to understand AIT and the information flooding his head, was suffering a delusion. He wasn't God's chosen messenger, and his death served no cosmic purpose."

Daniel's pulse quickened as he spoke, and his skin felt electric, and sweat broke out on his upper lip.

What if I passed out on Lexington Avenue and everything since then has been a dream?

What if this is all in my head?

He forced a slow breath, but his heart beat faster and a wave of vertigo washed through him. "Digger, how much of this is a delusion?" He reached for the balcony wall. "I'm not feeling very—"

"Stop! Be here now." Digger clunked the heel of her beer bottle hard on the back of his hand.

It hurt.

She said, "Feel that? This is real. Don't run away."

It worked, and the pain grounded him. He took a full breath and his pulse began to slow. "Ouch," he said.

"Don't make me do it again. I understand this Eckinsburger thing freaks you out—"

"*Daniel Byrne's coming to save us?* Yeah, it freaks me out. It feeds the same messianic delusion Tim suffered. And besides, I didn't apply for that job."

Digger smiled. "If it makes you feel any better, many of the lost souls in Source have predicted a savior. Eckinsburger probably just latched onto your name after Elias warned us to stay away from you. Understand, there've been dozens over time agitating for rebellion, talking of organizing a resistance movement. And some claimed visions of a"—she forced the word out—"*Noah*-level entity coming to oppose him. But you're not that. With practice, you might be a match for Elias . . . and Elias is powerful, but he's just a person like you and me."

Daniel said, "Are any of the agitators still—"

She shook her head. "Maybe he's got them up in the tower, maybe Elias killed them, but agitators are not tolerated. They just disappear. And he's got this place locked down to the point where we can't even meet in groups anymore. We get together in pairs now and then, take a walk or a swim, hang out for a couple of hours and talk. Sometimes manifest a meal and eat together, just because everything tastes so good here. But only in pairs. Any time we gather in groups of three or more, members of his flock show up and try to love-bomb us, telling us how great life is up in the tower, inviting us to join them. And always a couple of his soldiers come along, just so we get the message. And if he knows whenever we gather in groups, then he can see us. Maybe he can even hear us, if he's listening. I don't know."

"Why don't you all leave town, set up far away from here?"

"Can't leave town. Town goes on about ten miles from the ocean, then it just ends."

"Ends, how?"

"It's like a huge wall of glimmer, goes all the way up to the sky. Makes you sick, you can't even get close to it."

Daniel searched for a relatively benign question that would lead them back on track. He said, "What does he look like?"

"Like a normal man, except when he glims in and out of existence from one place to another. His power is incredible. He's not *God*-God, but everyone believes he's some kind of next-level entity. Because he is. Not God, but *a* god. If we felt like minor gods before he got here, the stuff he could do made us feel like nightclub magicians."

"So if he's a next-level entity, why didn't you follow him to the tower when he first arrived?"

"Because he's a dick, regardless of his power. I mean, if God turns out to be an asshole, should you still follow him? The day he arrived, he threw us a banquet and gave a big speech after dinner. Actually glimmed an entire restaurant into existence up the hill, linen tablecloths, fine china and silverware. Food on every plate, wine in every glass."

"Tuxedoed waiters?"

She shook her head. "Even he can't manifest any living thing above the consciousness level of plants. You can manifest a dead fish on a platter for dinner, but not a live fish."

"I noticed the lack of birds," said Daniel.

"No animals at all. Which sucks, because I'm a bit of a cat lady." She drank some beer. "Anyway, his basic message was that we were mistaken to think of Source as the source universe, or even a parallel reality. He said Source was the *only* reality, and Earth was just a dream we were having."

"But this place doesn't even hide its holographic nature, so how can he claim it's the only reality? How does he know there isn't another source universe projecting this one, and another behind that?"

She nodded. "And so on, and so on. It's turtles all the way down."

"Exactly."

"Of course it could be. We have no way of knowing. But human nature doesn't change by virtue of crossing over into Source. People are petrified of existential uncertainty, and he offered certainty."

"Particularly odd," said Daniel, "given that this place is a physical manifestation of the uncertainty principle."

She raised her bottle. "You're okay, Daniel Byrne. He'd never win you over."

"I've seen his grift before," Daniel said, remembering himself as a kid riding shotgun in the Winnebago with Tim Trinity. "Hell, I grew up in it. Sounds like Noah's running the same sort of con. He breezes into town performing his magic tricks and sells the snake oil of salvation through metaphysical certainty. It's the bromide at the root of every religious grift."

"Except," said Digger, "he does more than magic tricks. An example: When he arrived, there were about twelve hundred of us. None of us knew each other back on Earth, didn't know anything about each other. People arrived here with a clean slate, and we decided early on to respect that. It didn't matter who anyone was back home. Everyone got a new name, a new start. Here, people were who they said they were."

"You could just decide to be someone different, and no one would know," said Daniel.

"And I think many took it as an opportunity to reinvent themselves, leave a lot of emotional baggage back on Earth. But he arrived knowing us all. He knew our names on Earth, where we lived, what we did for a living. Every one of us. Which means he can see us back on Earth, too." She folded her arms across her chest, suppressing a shiver.

"Like a real god," she said.

16

Digger manifested crab cakes, warm in the oven, while Daniel manifested a Caesar salad and a bottle of dry rosé in the fridge. He couldn't decide between Bajan or Louisiana hot sauce, so he manifested both.

Over dinner on the balcony, she told him more of her life in Source before Noah's arrival, how Noah seduced the people here, how he intimidated those who resisted his charms and "disappeared" those who spoke out against him. She didn't use Noah's name—and neither did Daniel—but she acknowledged Daniel's need to know, and with some gentle prodding she answered his many questions as best she could.

"I have no idea," was a frequent answer, also a signal that his questions had again wandered away from the experience of Source and into the metaphysical woods. The woods where the minds of others in Source before him had wandered and gotten lost, never to find their way back.

A lot to take in.

Daniel closed his eyes and manifested a pot of coffee on the kitchen counter inside. He stood and collected their empty plates.

"Be right back," he said.

She called after him. "One cream, two sugars, please." When he paused, she added, "I can smell it."

He returned with the coffee, and they listened to the distant surf and sipped quietly for a minute. Despite the constant string of questions marching through Daniel's mind, he was getting better at *surfing the wave*—he sent a silent thanks to his friend Natty B—and now he could feel Digger's presence from across the table.

She'd said people learn to feel the presence of others nearby in Source, that you could tap into their emotional state. And it was true. It was like Daniel could feel a muted sense of what she was feeling, not the way you infer another's mood from body language and tone, but a direct feeling, coming across the table like heat from a radiator.

She was cautious more than fearful, her caution directed toward the tower in the distance, keeping herself on alert. But there was also a certain defiant pride, and a sense of camaraderie with Daniel. He couldn't read her thoughts, but her emotional state was clear.

Daniel marveled at the intimacy of it, and he thought of Kara. She'd had AIT. Maybe she could learn to cross over. He allowed himself the brief fantasy of exploring Source with Kara, then shut it down.

He said, "Aside from Noah, I do love it here. I realize that's like saying, *Aside from that, Mrs. Lincoln, how was the play?* but I can't get over the potential of this place. It's incredible."

"You're a natural," said Digger, raising her coffee mug. "This is one strongly intentioned cup o' joe."

"Glad you approve."

"No, really. Nobody's first coffee tastes this good. They always start off a bit generic." She put her mug down and looked straight at Daniel. "That's why he wants you dead."

"He must really hate coffee," said Daniel.

She shot him a look. "Listen. You've done things on your first attempt that take everybody else a hundred tries or more."

"The things we can do here," said Daniel, "as weird as it is to admit . . . they feel almost natural to me."

"That's because—" She caught herself, started over. "My theory is, navigating in Source feels natural to you because your consciousness has been here before, only you don't know it."

"That's not a theory, it's just a guess."

"Look at the evidence. Exhibit A: You do things here like you've done them many times before. Exhibit B: You told me you had an apartment, complete with personal belongings, already manifested when you arrived. The rest of us had only the clothes on our backs. You see? You've been here all along. You just can't remember. An apartment, for God's sake. Nobody else. You're the only one."

Daniel pointed his coffee mug at Noah's white tower. "I suspect he's got a pretty swingin' pad up there."

"Well, right. You didn't manifest a four-hundred-story skyscraper on your first day. Noah's a next-level entity. Like I said before, you're not one of him, you're one of us. But you're the most powerful one of us I've ever seen. Now that your entire consciousness is here, and with a little practice . . . Look. Head-to-head, he'd make short work of you and be back to his breakfast before his eggs got cold. I haven't changed on that. But maybe you could be powerful enough to toss a monkey wrench into his intentions, after all. Maybe he thought it prudent to take you out prophylactically, if you'll pardon the word choice."

"Maybe," said Daniel. "But we don't even know what his intentions are." He looked back to the tower in the distance. "What do two thousand people do up there all day?"

"I've never been, but they say the bottom 350 floors are empty. Say they spend a lot of time meditating on the top floor of the building and Noah lives up on the roof, in the glim, but he guides their meditations. And they say he gives talks—sermons, I guess. He's got them convinced that Earth is a dream, and they're somehow making it a better dream."

Daniel remembered the first time he saw the tower. He'd thought the sun was reflecting off a glass wall on the penthouse level. But it wasn't sunlight reflecting off glass. It was, as they called it in Source, the glim. Atop a tower built by Noah's *intentions*.

How do you go up against a guy like that?

Daniel said, "How close do you think we can get before we give ourselves away? I'd like to take a—"

Digger was rising from her chair, staring past Daniel, terror in her eyes, staring away from Noah's tower, pointing down toward the beach.

It had been a clear day since they'd arrived, but now a large storm front hung low in the western sky, over the ocean, a few hundred yards from landfall, thick black clouds moving toward shore, gray curtains of rain sheeting down to the water below.

"Shit," said Digger.

The clouds billowed up, growing so fast they looked like a time-lapse video, rolling and billowing until they blocked the bottom half of the sun.

Like turning a dimmer switch on the world.

She said, "We have to get back home."

Back home. Daniel remembered. *I'm in a float tank in Barcelona. How could I have forgotten that?*

"Damn it," she said, "we shouldn't have talked about him. He knows where we are. We have to move."

"Wait, he knows where we are here, or—you said he can see people on Earth. Is the risk here, or there? Where's the danger?"

"I don't know." She stepped forward. "And there's less difference between the two than you might think." She touched his arm. "Remember the float spa. Picture yourself there, remember how it felt just before you lost track of your body and crossed over. The air in the float tank smells of salt, remember that smell. Close your eyes, feel yourself there, and you'll be there. I'll see you back home."

Daniel stole a glance back at the storm as it rolled in, picking up speed, reaching the shore and rising even higher, blotting out more sunlight, darkening the world.

"Go," said Digger, her eyes flicking back at the storm. "I'll buy you time."

"No, you come, too. We go at the same time."

"It's not up for debate." She grabbed Daniel's arms and spun him away. "I'll be right behind you. Now go!"

Daniel closed his eyes.

I'm in Barcelona, Spain.

In a float tank.

The air is salty.

17

D aniel let out the breath he was holding and filled his lungs again.

He opened his eyes.

He was nowhere.

Caught between worlds? Trapped in a void? Dead? His mind grasped for context.

No light, no sound, no—

Wait. The air is salty.

Float tank in Barcelona.

He moved his arms and heard water splash. He contracted his stomach, feeling for which way was up, then sat up and blindly reached his right arm out until it touched the smooth wall.

He ran his hand along the wall until it found the switch. The LEDs in the ceiling came alive, and he was bathed in blue light. He pressed the red button, and the hatch door rose on pneumatic hinges.

Daniel stepped down from the tank and into the bright room, still feeling disoriented. He knew he was in the float spa in Barcelona but he'd been in another place, and the memory was returning fragmented. He remembered the sand between his toes, the sun frozen in the sky. Source—he'd been in Source—with . . . Digger. She'd taught him how to spot-travel. They'd had dinner— crab cakes—on a balcony. Something had gone wrong, something about a storm . . .

Pat was leaning against the far wall, by the door, working the crossword on a folded newspaper. He lowered the paper as Daniel wrapped himself in one of the thick bathrobes supplied by the float spa.

"Didn't work, huh?"

Daniel shook his head. "It worked plenty."

"But you guys just got in."

"No, I—we were there half a day."

Pat shook his head, confirmed it with a glance at his watch. "You've been in there just under four and a half minutes."

Digger's words came back to him: *Time works differently here.* He let out a low whistle. "Digger wasn't kidding."

"Digger?"

"Dr. Cameron. That's what she's called there—in Source."

Then Daniel remembered. It all came flooding back.

He knows where we are.

I'll buy you time.

"Dude, we gotta motor."

"Relax," said Pat, "we're cool. Nobody's arrived since you went in. Pretty Boy at the counter's just lookin' bored, reading *GQ* and practic- ing his pout. Only thing's changed: He put on a Santa hat. I think he thinks he's being ironic."

"You don't understand, Noah's a—I don't know exactly what Noah is, but he's bad business. He knows what everyone in Source is named on Earth, what everyone does for a living, where they live—that's how Elias knew where to find me in Barbados."

"You mean Drapeau."

Daniel nodded as he strode across to Digger's float tank. "Same guy. I don't know if Noah knows where we are right this instant, but he very well might—he found us there in less than five minutes, Earth time. Digger's right; he's some next-level entity. He built a four-hundred-story skyscraper out of pure intention and—"

"Slow down." Pat eyed Daniel for a second before speaking. "I gotta level with you, Dan. You're not sounding strictly one hundred percent rational right now. But if you say we gotta motor, we motor." He nodded at the closed float tank. "You're the AIT expert. Any idea how we wake the professor?"

"That's the problem. Forcing someone out of an AIT episode is a high-risk play—it can trigger a severe dissociative state with crippling and long-term mental health repercussions. Sometimes permanent. It's just something you don't do." Daniel thought back to what he'd learned from Ayo Onatade, head of the Foundation's AIT team. The risk of triggering such a state was about five percent. One in twenty.

Pat said, "So we give her a little more time. She knows what she's doing."

Daniel looked at the float tank. Cameron did know what she was doing. She was a capable woman with an agile mind. She'd been in Source through Noah's ascendency, remained an independent straggler, in defiance of his wishes, while the vast majority became his flock and those who spoke against him vanished. She'd walked that tightrope and survived. She couldn't toss dumpsters around, but she'd outwitted a professional assassin, saving Daniel's life. Probably saved his life again, just moments ago. Waking her might destroy her mind, but not waking her . . .

He did the math. They'd been at the float spa for twenty-three minutes, the university a couple hours before, but Daniel and Pat had conducted a twenty-four-hour surveillance on Cameron, sleeping in shifts, to be sure Drapeau wasn't hanging around in the shadows before Daniel made his approach. In total, Daniel had been in Barcelona for almost thirty straight hours. Seemed an unsafe length of time to stay in one place, considering Noah's special talent.

Is the risk here, or there?

There's less difference between the two than you might think.

"No," said Daniel. "We have to risk it. I'm gonna wake her."

"You're the boss. I'll check our exit, you get her up and get dressed."

Pat left the room and Daniel returned to the float tank. He opened the hatch, reaching inside to flip on the blue lights.

Dana Cameron lay floating.

Unmoving.

Facedown.

Daniel launched himself halfway into the tank, grabbing an ankle, a knee, pulling her closer, hooking one arm around her ribcage and hauling her through the hatch, tumbling to the floor beside her.

He scrambled to his feet against the weight of his waterlogged bathrobe, got hold of her legs and lifted high, until salt water flowed from her lungs, out her mouth, onto the floor.

He put her legs down and flipped her onto her back. She didn't cough, didn't gasp, didn't move at all. Her eyes stared up at the ceiling, unblinking, seeing nothing.

Daniel blew four breaths into her lungs. Felt for a pulse.

No pulse.

Pat walked through the door as Daniel made a fist and pounded the Flash logo on Dana Cameron's chest.

"Fuck me," said Pat, dropping to his knees and taking over mouth-to-mouth as Daniel started CPR.

Pat paused every four breaths and felt for a pulse. And at some point, he just stopped. But Daniel didn't stop until Pat reached out and touched his arm.

"The woman ain't coming back, brother. I'm sorry. She's a rag doll, zero muscle tension, been dead for some minutes. Probably before you even climbed out of your tank."

Daniel leaned on one elbow and caught his breath, unable to look away from Cameron's dead eyes. He'd barely known her, but he liked her. She'd been smart and funny and brave. Risked her life to save his, to guide him into Source. He felt like he'd lost a friend.

The wave of grief rolled over him, leaving behind a more selfish thought:

She had so much more to tell me.

And then the guilt.

He leaned forward and closed her eyelids.

Pat said, "We need a head start outta here. She's gotta go back in. Get dressed."

Daniel dropped the sopping bathrobe on the floor and climbed into his clothes, as Pat lifted Dana Cameron's body, carried it over to the tank, and floated it, as gently as possible, faceup in the salt water.

Pat closed the hatch. "Ready?"

Daniel shoved his pistol in one pocket, cell phone in another, and nodded. He followed Pat out the door and into the reception area.

The bored young man at the counter looked up as they passed, and in one smooth motion, Pat raised a silenced pistol and pointed it straight at the white felt band of his Santa hat and—

Daniel grabbed the gun and pivoted, walking into Pat and raising his arm. They stood chest to chest, both holding the gun high.

Pat could've easily overpowered Daniel, but instead he said, "Well, this is awkward."

"A little," said Daniel.

"So . . . you gonna let me do my job?"

Daniel said, "Just . . . hold that thought." He turned to face the young man, who stood frozen and trembling behind the counter.

He said, "You want to live, right?"

18

W hat the hell were you thinking?" barked Pat. He slowed and turned the corner onto one of Barcelona's wide, tree-lined boulevards, then put on some speed, blending into the flow of traffic.

"I was thinking: *Maybe let's not shoot the innocent bystander.* Have you lost your mind?"

"No." Pat challenged Daniel with a sharp glare. "Have you?" He returned his eyes to the road, but he wasn't done. "Soon as Pretty Boy frees himself, he'll be describing us to the cops, and they'll nab us trying to leave the country. Use your head. He's the only thing that connects us with the professor's body."

Pat was right about that. Daniel would be on the university's security footage, but they'd parked the car on a small side street—a dead zone a few blocks from campus. Cameron had left her office building ten minutes after Daniel, by a different exit. No traffic cameras on the float spa's block, and no CCTV inside the spa.

But Pat was also wrong.

"Yes, he's the only thing that connects us," said Daniel. "Only, he isn't a *thing*."

"All wars include collateral damage," said Pat.

A sense-memory washed over Daniel—the coppery taste of Kara's blood filling his mouth as he breathed air into her punctured lung, his finger plugging the hole between her ribs—and with it came the overwhelming sense of helplessness, the despair, and the rage.

He forced the memory away. "I'm sick of collateral damage," he said. "And ends justifying means is a slippery slope. I don't like where it leads."

"That's pretty rich coming from a guy who committed premeditated murder a few months back."

"Conrad Winter wasn't innocent."

"No shit, Sherlock. You did the world a favor. There is such a thing as a righteous murder. But I've been a soldier all my adult life, all over the world. What I've learned? Nobody's fuckin' *innocent.*"

Daniel waved it away. "That's a cynical pose and you know it. Mercenary friend once told me, 'Scratch any cynic, you find a wounded idealist underneath.' Oh, right. It was you."

Pat smiled, but it was a sad smile. "Not anymore, brother." He lowered the window and lit a smoke. "Maybe I've just seen too much of the shit, I don't know. Bottom line: Most people are just no damn good."

"You think that kid deserved to die for having bad taste in hairstyles and working a part-time job in a float spa? Really?" Daniel pulled the burner phone from his pocket. "We'll grab the next commuter flight to anywhere, be out of the country by the time he frees himself. I'm good at knots. And you know what else?" He flashed Pat the driver's license he'd taken from the kid. "He's convinced we'll come find him and punch his ticket if he describes us accurately to the cops. So he'll tell himself he doesn't remember clearly, blame the stress, his memory will accidentally on purpose grow hazy, and he'll misremember enough details that his description to the cops won't look like us."

"You hope," said Pat.

Daniel turned and looked out the window. He said, "While we're on the subject of collateral damage: Digger didn't want to talk about Noah, and I pushed her until she relented. And then he found us. I got her killed."

"Correlation does not imply causation," said Pat.

"Oh, fuck off," said Daniel.

"You fuck off," said Pat. "You don't know that's why Noah found you. You said time moves a lot slower there. He had hours to notice you. Maybe you got her killed, maybe not, but you can't know that. From where I'm sitting, your guilt looks a little like self-indulgence. And I say that with love. I know you're going through a lot of weird mental shit, but you really gotta try and keep your head in the game."

The next few miles out of the city passed in silence, Pat smoking and Daniel searching airline schedules on his burner phone. As they approached the highway, Pat tossed his cigarette butt and raised the window. He said, "You gonna tell me what happened, or I gotta ask?"

Daniel said, "Let's stipulate up front: It sounds crazy. I know it sounds crazy, so that's not the kind of feedback I'm looking for."

"Scout's honor," said Pat.

"Okay. She was right—it's not a vision, it's a place. The people who can cross over from here to there call it Source."

"A place where? Like a parallel universe?"

"Maybe. I don't know, and I don't want to get into metaphors. Nobody there really knows what it is, though most think they do.

They've been seduced into believing that Source is the only reality"—
he gestured to the Spanish countryside all around—"and *this* is just
a dream."

"Some dream," said Pat.

Then Daniel told Pat the rest, everything Dana Cameron had
told him, all he had seen and done in Source, the hyper-real textures
and tastes, the ability to manifest things from nothing, to spot-travel
from one place to another.

When Daniel finished, Pat said, "Tell you what, if this Noah char-
acter wants to make Earth a better dream, he can be my guest."

"Dude. He rules Source with an iron fist, makes agitators
disappear—look what he did to the professor, just because she
showed me a different perspective. That's not how you make the
dream better."

Pat shrugged. "Depends on how great he thinks the better dream
can be. You know that cliché about omelets and eggs. Maybe he looks
around at the shitty dream we got, and he decides the ends really do
justify the means."

Daniel said, "First of all, Earth is not a dream." The ghost of an ice
cube slid down his spine as he said it. "Although I gotta admit, Source
feels every bit as real as this place. More real, to be honest."

"Wouldn't surprise me," said Pat. "I've always suspected we're
livin' in a kind of dream, ever since I was a kid."

They rode in silence for a minute.

Daniel said, "When I was nine years old, Tim quit the tent revival
circuit for the summer and we stayed put in New Orleans. He got me
a dog at the SPCA on Japonica Street, and he insisted on naming it
Judas. He thought that was hilarious. We were walking in Audubon

Park—it was over a hundred degrees out and Judas was straining at his leash, wanted to cool off in the big water fountain. Tim let him off the leash and he ran ahead, maybe a hundred yards, jumped in the fountain. And I stood there, watching him splash around, and I thought, *I can see the fountain from here. I can close my eyes, and in my mind I can be standing right there at the fountain, patting Judas, and I know what wet dog feels like. I can put my mind there, so why can't I just put my body there, too?*"

"Ha! You wanted to spot-travel."

"Exactly. And this thought—this feeling that if you can *see* a place, you should just be able to *be* there—stayed with me for, I don't know, ten years maybe. Practically every time I walked somewhere, I had it again. Some time in my late teens, it just went away, and I forgot all about it. Until just this minute."

Pat said, "Maybe the professor was right. Maybe part of your consciousness was in Source all along, and you just brought that desire to spot-travel into the dream."

"Except this isn't a dream. Parallel reality maybe, but not a dream. I can't believe that."

"Why not?"

"Because believing Earth is a dream means the people around you aren't real, they're just characters in your dream. And that leads to solipsism, and solipsist is just a fancy word for sociopath. It's a philosophy that denies other people their free will, destroys empathy."

Pat laughed. "Don't you keep up on science? There ain't no such thing as *free will*. They proved it, hooked folks up to brain scans. Know what they found? We make choices so fast we ain't even making them. Show someone two options, and boom"—he snapped his fingers—"choice is made. Then, *afterwards*, we go through the process of rationalizing, pretending we're carefully considering our options and being smart. Truth is, choice was made before we even knew there was a choice in front of us. Free will is an illusion, man."

Daniel thought about that. He said, "There was a famous rabbi, I don't remember his name, who said, 'I don't believe in God because there is one, I believe in God because there should be.' I guess that's how I feel about free will."

"Fine. You go on, keep your head in the sand, but it ain't just science that proves me right. It's also experience. I look around, and I see the world populated by robots and zombies, every last one of us. And our need to think we got free will makes us easy to manipulate. All you gotta do is create a painful situation, then offer an escape from the pain. Make it a binary choice, people will take the easy way out. They'll go where you want them to go, do what you want them to do, every damn time. And the best part? You make them work for it, just a bit, and they'll be absolutely convinced they *chose* that path of their own free will."

"You must be a hell of a lot of fun at parties," said Daniel.

"All I'm saying is, human beings are hardwired all wrong. We're doomed by our DNA, destined to treat each other like shit. If a giant alien spaceship entered our atmosphere tomorrow morning and a booming voice said, 'We have crossed a vast distance from planet Don't Be An Asshole, and we will now vaporize planet Earth if you don't stop being assholes to each other,' we couldn't do it. We wouldn't last an hour."

"We're not fallen angels, Pat. We're risen apes. Human history is written in blood, but we're getting better."

"Not better enough."

Daniel said, "You say most people are no damn good, but I know you know better. The real bad guys are a small minority—"

"And you know why that doesn't matter?" said Pat.

"Oh, here we go," Daniel sighed.

"Because the so-called good guys won't do what it takes to win, won't allow the ends to justify the means. They gotta preserve their sense of moral purity, so they put limits on their behavior and always end up losing to the bad guys, who have no problem doing whatever it takes to win."

"It's not about moral purity," said Daniel. "It's about not becoming what you're fighting against."

"Oh boo-fucking-hoo. Life sucks and then you die." Pat sent Daniel a grin. "And before you start to think I'm fixin' to throw myself off a tall building, I will now share with you the *good* news."

"If you hand me a *Watchtower*, we are not friends anymore."

Pat laughed. "Nah, the good news is—okay, I'm sure Raoul's head would explode if he knew I was sharin' this, but I think you need to know: AIT has passed the 500,000 mark. Spreading so fast it'll be a million before the ball drops on Times Square."

"Holy shit."

"You said it."

"And how is this good news?"

"You know, maybe AIT represents some kinda jump in human evolution. Maybe it'll fix what's broken in our DNA and we'll all end up holdin' hands, singing 'Kumbaya.'"

Then Pat started singing.

"Okay, now you're just messin'."

Pat howled with laughter. "Gotta keep your sense of humor intact."

They rolled on in silence for a few miles.

Then Pat said, "You really think this Noah can find you here, with his *mind*?"

"He can build a four-hundred-story skyscraper with his mind, I'd say it's a pretty safe bet he can find me here if he tries. He knows where everyone in Source lives on Earth, knows details about their lives. And no one tested my legend before Drapeau came for me in Barbados. I'm guessing Noah told him where to find me."

"Damn, son. That's not good."

"It is precisely double-plus ungood," said Daniel.

"So what's the plan?"

Daniel looked at his watch and let out a long breath. He leaned back against the headrest with his eyes closed, trying not to see Dana Cameron's dead body sprawled on the floor of the float spa. He rubbed his temples, taking deep decompression breaths. He'd been back almost two hours, but he didn't quite feel present, almost like he'd left part of himself in Source.

Yet another absurdity that simply felt true.

Wait. Is that the taste of cinnamon?

He opened his eyes. Pat sat behind the wheel, chewing gum.

"Is that cinnamon flavored?"

Pat stopped chewing. "Oh, shit. Sorry, I didn't think." He cracked the window and tossed the gum out. "Won't happen again."

"Yeah, better if it didn't," said Daniel. "Having enough trouble hanging onto reality . . . whatever the hell reality is." He took another deep breath, refocusing on practical matters.

After a minute, he said, "Okay, I've got the plan. Remember what you said about the relative merits of mobility and battlements?"

"Yup."

"The plan is to keep moving until we think of a plan."

19

So they kept moving. A nonstop flight to Paris on Air France, followed by a CityJet flight to London, then changing planes for a connecting flight to Antwerp.

In every departure lounge, television screens played scenes of angry public protests spreading around the world, and huge displays of *The Truth (So Far) about Trinity* stood at the entrance of every airport bookstore and sundry shop, and everywhere Daniel looked, he saw posters advertising the book.

The posters featured the headline READ THE BOOK THAT'S CHANGING THE WORLD, above a photo of the book and a larger picture of Julia, smiling into the camera lens.

Daniel was struck by how little Poster-Julia looked like herself, the smile lines beside her eyes and the frown line in the middle of her forehead all Photoshopped out of existence. Clearly, her publisher's advertising department believed the book that's changing the world should've been written by a younger version of Julia.

Nice priorities, thought Daniel.

In Antwerp, Pat and Daniel used new passports to rent a Mercedes sedan, and then hit the highway, driving an hour south through the black Belgian night.

It was just after two a.m. when they stopped in downtown Brussels, at La Porte Noire, an old basement cellar bar with vaulted brick ceilings, over a hundred different beers, and live music by a band called the Narcotic Daffodils.

The music was good, the cheese plate and beer absolutely necessary. On the run since midday yesterday—five cities in four countries in fourteen hours—Daniel was running ragged. And tomorrow they'd fly to Dusseldorf, rent another car and head north, changing passports again for the border, and drop that car in Amsterdam. Then fly to . . . hell, might as well fly to the moon.

"This is not a sustainable plan," Daniel said. "I have to cross over."

"What?"

"I have to go back to Source."

"That doesn't sound like a better plan," said Pat. "You *think* Noah can find you here, but you *know* he can find you there. He got to the professor in Source, even with all her experience there. What makes you think he won't find you?"

"He will." Daniel took a swig of beer. "But you're wrong—I do know he can find me here. He sent Drapeau for me in Barbados—I'm sure of it. The question isn't whether he can find me, it's how long it takes him after he starts looking. Like we've said, time moves slower there—I mean a *lot* slower. We were only in the float tanks four and a half minutes, but in Source we were there for hours. We got a lot done in that time. So the plan is: I go back, poke around, get near the tower, see what I can learn. Maybe I'll run into one of the other Independents, who knows?"

"Pretty big risk for *who knows*."

"No choice. To beat your enemy, you must understand what your enemy wants. Yes?"

"Yes."

"I can't learn that here. So I go back, ready to bug out as soon as I see a raincloud."

Pat drank some bottled water. "Your call. But do me a favor and err on the side of getting back early. Don't make me haul your corpse out of a float tank."

Daniel raised his beer bottle. "Scout's honor." He took a swig. "Anyway, I don't need a float tank."

"She said it works faster in water. You're gonna want to come and go quickly."

"Don't need it," said Daniel. He didn't know how he knew this, but he was absolutely certain. Something in him had changed in Source, and he knew crossing over would now be as easy as—a manic energy rose in his chest as he thought it, thrilled by the prospect of going back—as easy as spot-traveling. He said, "We'll do it in the car. I'll cross over from the seat, and you keep us a moving target."

✢ ✢ ✢

Daniel paused again, his finger hovering over Send. He read the email a third time.

Hey, You—

I'm really sorry it's taken me so long to get in touch. Big developments with my AIT, and the life I thought I'd left behind has proven harder to leave behind than I'd anticipated. Wish I could tell you everything that's going on, but it would take more time than I have. Things are complicated right now. Please understand, my feelings haven't changed: I can't wait to see you, touch you, hear your news and tell you mine, hear your laugh again. I meant every-thing I said before, and I'm asking you to hang on while I *uncomplicate* things. I know it's a lot to ask, and I wish I didn't have to ask it. But I do.

Stay well, and I'll be in touch as soon as I can.

Love,
Me

PS: This email address is a one-time deal, so don't reply. Respond by usual method. Will check it when I can.

It sucked, but Daniel couldn't think how to fix it. He hit Send. And as soon as it was gone, he worried that he'd used all the wrong words.

"*Things are complicated*"? *Idiot.*

He fought the urge to write a quick follow-up to clarify that *complicated* didn't mean another romantic relationship. They'd made no promise of exclusivity, but he wanted Kara to know he wasn't playing the field in her absence. He decided he was being paranoid—she'd be rightly pissed that he'd been so vague, but she wouldn't look for hidden meaning in it.

He put the phone away as Pat returned to the car and handed him a large coffee.

Pat started the engine and popped a caffeine pill. "Want one?" He put the pills away when Daniel shook his head, and pulled back onto the highway, away from the rest stop's oasis of light, and into the dark night. "So how do we do this?"

Daniel took a sip of coffee and put the paper cup in the armrest holder. He pushed the button to recline his seat and closed his eyes. "Stay on the E40 toward Leuven, keep the radio off, and don't chew gum. I'll be back before my coffee gets cold."

"You got it."

Daniel opened his eyes. "And do not wake me unless we're under attack."

"Yeah, dissociative state, I remember."

Daniel leaned back, closed his eyes, and folded his hands across his chest.

20

D aniel let out the breath he was holding and filled his lungs again. He was standing in the bedroom of his apartment in Source, just as he'd visualized.

Red walls, the same shade as his childhood home in New Orleans, and the same cedar armoire with the white porcelain knobs that had been in Tim's room. He spotted the waxed leather shoes on the floor. His shoes, perfectly formed to his feet by many wearings in Source.

Digger's theory, that Daniel had been here all along but just couldn't remember, was the most reasonable explanation he could find. Once again, he had to face it: In Source, the fact that something was completely absurd did not make it untrue.

Which should be no surprise, since the entire human condition back on Earth was absurd. The difference being, on Earth, there were so many ways to distract yourself from this existential fact. Here it just refused to be ignored.

But if Source really was the fundamental reality, as people here supposed, then this apartment had existed here first. Had Daniel simply projected familiar details from his life in Source—the cedar armoire, the red walls, the rug in the living room—into the dream of his life on Earth, as Noah preached?

That way lies madness. Daniel drew a deep breath.

Union with the wave.

Be here now.

Surf.

A few deep breaths cleared his mind. He sat on the edge of the bed and changed into his Source shoes. He stood and closed his eyes, visualized his Sig in the nightstand until he felt the shift, then opened the drawer and withdrew the gun, popping the mag to confirm it was, indeed, loaded. He reinserted the mag and tucked the gun behind his belt. He closed the drawer and did it again, this time manifesting a Sharpie.

He wrote BREATHE on the palm of his left hand, then walked through the living room, crossing Kara Singh's antique rug—or the rug he dreamed was Kara's—and opened the balcony doors. The sun hung in the western sky as before, not a cloud to be seen.

He picked a spot on the patio two floors below, focused on it. Thinking: *If you can see a place, you can be there.* He closed his eyes and saw himself standing below, occupying that space. Felt the shift. Opened his eyes.

He was standing down on the patio. He remembered to breathe without reading his hand—the act of writing it down had been enough to lodge it in his mind.

Looking ahead, Daniel picked another spot almost a block up the road.

And spot-traveled again.

And again.

And again.

He glanced back to his balcony. He'd traveled three blocks in under ten seconds.

He was good at this.

A few blocks later, he decided on a bigger challenge. He visualized a dumpster in the alley around the corner. Waited for the shift, and felt it. He turned the corner to see his handiwork.

It wasn't a dumpster. It wasn't even close to a dumpster. It was more like a hunk of scrap metal, grossly misshapen, and it was only the size of a shopping cart.

Daniel shrugged off the disappointment. It was his first try. With practice, he'd get there. He turned his attention back to spot-traveling through town.

He stopped when a sudden chill ran down his arms, followed by a tingle on the top of his scalp. This was the feeling Dana Cameron had described—the feeling of someone's presence nearby. He thought back to what she'd told him and put his attention on the feeling.

It seemed to come from behind him.

He turned around and faced the empty street.

The tingling subsided, replaced by . . . what? A feeling of curiosity, but not his own. Someone else's curiosity about him? That felt true. The curiosity was restrained by caution, bordering on fear. And behind those two feelings was a deep and abiding sadness.

Daniel felt certain he was reading these feelings accurately. Curiosity, caution, sadness.

Whoever this was, it wasn't Elias.

"I'm not with Noah," he said to the empty street. "My name is Daniel Byrne."

From around the corner walked a boy. About twelve, thin but not underfed, a mop of sandy hair hanging in his eyes, clothes and face a bit dirty—but the kind of dirty a boy gets after a day of outdoor adventure, not the kind that speaks of poverty or neglect. He wore blue jeans and a red T-shirt with the Flash logo on the chest. The boy walked forward tentatively, stopped with more than a dozen feet between them, and brushed the hair out of his eyes.

"I know who you are. Everyone here knows." The boy looked at the ground. "Digger's dead, isn't she?"

"Yes," said Daniel. "I'm sorry, she is."

The boy blinked hard a couple of times, got it under control, and jammed his hands in his pockets. "Fuck."

"She give you that shirt?"

The boy nodded at the ground. "She was my friend. She looked out for me the most."

Daniel wanted to approach the boy and put a hand on his shoulder. But he didn't. With Digger's death confirmed, the boy was now mostly sadness and fear, curiosity plummeting.

"Son, what's your name?"

The boy spoke without looking up. "My Earth name is George. People here call me Huck, but I never read the book. Anyway, I like it better than George."

"It's a good name," said Daniel. "How did you know Digger died, Huck?"

Huck continued talking to the pavement. "She told me she was gonna try and help you, said I should stay away for a bit, to be safe, 'cause Elias don't want anyone talking to you. I saw you guys walking on the beach, but I stayed away like she said. Then the storm came and I hid in a basement." He looked up, finally, and held Daniel's gaze. "I hope you're worth it."

A mix of grief and guilt knotted Daniel's gut, and he swallowed to clear the lump in his throat. "I hope so, too," he said.

Huck watched Daniel for a moment without speaking, and Daniel realized the boy was tapping into his feelings, reading him. Finally the boy said, "You gonna help us? You gonna save us from Noah?"

"Not sure I can, Huck," said Daniel. "I'm gonna try. But I think Digger was right. Probably best if you try to stay on Earth for a bit. You should be back with your folks."

Huck shook his head. He looked away for a few seconds, deciding. He said, "You know how Noah says Earth is just a dream?"

"Digger told me."

"Well, my dream was a shithole basement apartment full of cockroaches in Kokomo, Indiana. My parents were junkies. They blew the place up trying to cook meth one day when I was at school. First grade. They went to jail and I bounced around foster homes ever since. So my dream life on Earth ain't much worth dreaming. Way I figure it, Source is probably just another dream, but at least it was a good one till Noah showed up and wrecked everything. Besides, I can look after myself better here. I don't need money, I can manifest new clothes whenever I need, or a soccer ball when I'm bored."

"Are there other kids here?"

"They all went to live in the tower, but the grown-ups who stayed indie are nice. Wish I could see them more. Anyway, save your breath. Earth sucks. Here, I'm on an adventure, even when it's scary. I don't go back to Earth anymore and I never will, no matter what happens." Huck shot a nervous glance at the white tower in the distance. "I'm gonna split. Two together doesn't usually draw them out, but after what—after Digger . . ."

Daniel nodded. "Keep your head down, y'hear?"

"I will." Huck shifted foot to foot. "Good luck."

Daniel stepped forward, shook the boy's hand. "You're a good man, Huck. Stay safe."

21

D aniel extended the brass telescope to full length, thinking:
Arr, matey! Manifested meself a pirate's spyglass, I have.

Only, he hadn't visualized a telescope he'd ever seen in the material world. He'd manifested the spyglass of Billy Bones, from the copy of *Treasure Island* he'd read and re-read as a child. The telescope he'd imagined, while immersed in the book and imagining himself as young Jim Hawkins.

Daniel's personal Platonic form of a pirate's telescope, in physical form.

It really is all just a dance of energy and information.

Shit. Daniel collapsed the scope, his heart picking up speed, skin electric. He could not afford a rush right now, but clearly some part of his mind wanted off this ride. He stood frozen, consumed by dread, as he caught the faint smell of coffee in the distance.

Coffee.

In a car.

In Belgium.

Was he there, or here? Was he dreaming right now? Or was Earth a dream . . . or both . . . or were they both real, or—?

Now coffee was joined by another scent—the new car smell of the rented Mercedes. A cold sweat broke out on Daniel's forehead and the world began to shimmer and he became dizzy, his moorings slipping.

No, no, no. Be here now.

He drew a long, slow breath through his nose, held it, then pushed it out through pursed lips.

And again.

And again, turning the spyglass around in his hands, feeling the cool, smooth brass, feeling the weight of the thing.

Thinking: *This is solid.*

Thinking: *Surf the wave.*

Whatever Earth was, he reminded himself, this place was real and he'd only made progress by surfing the wave. After parting ways with Huck, he'd focused on spot-traveling, pushing his limits with each jump, and he was now able to travel three blocks at a go. And he'd successfully manifested a dumpster—admittedly, about half the size of a normal dumpster, but normal in all other respects. And now he stood on the rooftop of a four-story apartment building, less than two blocks from Noah's tower, with line of sight to the main entrance.

He scanned the sky in all directions—a sheet of blue, no cloud anywhere. If weather was the indicator, Noah's attention was not currently focused on Daniel's whereabouts. He took another deep breath as his heart rate decreased. The coffee aroma had dissipated, and he was surfing again, in the now.

He raised the scope to his eye and pointed it at Noah's front door. He'd positioned himself with the sun behind the tower, and he could see inside well enough.

A glass wall fronted the tower's airy modern lobby. The floor and pillars and reception desk were clad in white marble, a black marble water fountain providing contrast. Daniel could see part of a sitting area—chrome and smoked glass tables, white leather Barcelona chairs and couches.

This was the first impression Noah presented to newcomers. Not exactly Saint Peter at the pearly gates, but Noah wasn't selling the premise that they'd arrived in heaven, just that they were finally awake.

Daniel panned the scope back through the lobby.

Nobody home.

He raised the spyglass, scanning each floor along the way. All empty, and he remembered Digger telling him the bottom 350 floors were vacant. He held the glass level and looked into the floor directly across. The entire floor was open—interior walls only finishing the stairwells and elevator banks and support beams—ready to be framed into luxury apartments or Spartan dormitories, meditation halls or dining halls, schoolrooms . . . whatever Noah decided, as more people crossed over to Source—or woke up.

Or maybe Noah hadn't built the tower so tall in anticipation of increased population. Maybe its height was simply intended to strike awe in the hearts of the population already here when Noah arrived.

A simple and overwhelming display of power, not lost on Daniel.

His fear now told him entering the tower was a suicide mission. It forced him to remember his existence in a car in Belgium, insisted he cross over, now. But by facing the fear directly and thinking it through, Daniel found he could abort the adrenaline rush. So he thought it through.

Bottom line: He could not face off against Noah without knowing more, and he couldn't learn more without entering the tower. He had to face the fear and do it anyway.

If not now, when?

This truly would be a suicide mission, however, if he allowed his fear to come with him into that tower. Daniel kneeled on the rooftop and sat on his heels. He put the telescope to one side, straightened his posture, and made his hands into a Zen mudra in his lap.

He let his gaze fall, unfocused, to a patch of rooftop four feet ahead and spent a couple minutes counting breaths, then moving beyond counting, beyond breath itself, until there were no thoughts, only awareness.

After abiding in stillness for a few minutes, Daniel finished his brief meditation with:

Today is a good day to die. But I've decided to stay alive until tomorrow.

He stood and stepped to the rooftop's edge, looking straight across, into Noah's tower. Distance: about one and a half blocks. Daniel could easily do three.

There was, however, a double-pane window between Daniel and his intended destination. Would that make a difference? An image— Daniel re-manifesting outside the window, pedaling the air like Wile E. Coyote—came to mind unbidden, and he felt himself smile. The meditation had done its job.

He focused his attention on a spot beside the stairwell door, about twenty feet beyond the window.

If you can see a place, you can be there.

✤ ✤ ✤

It worked.

Looking back across the empty interior of the tower, through the window, to the rooftop from whence he came, Daniel experienced a sense of pure wonder and undiluted joy. For a moment, he allowed himself to imagine what Source could be, post-Noah.

Once again, he ached to show Kara this place, to explore its potential together.

Post-Noah.

Daniel cleared his mind and entered the stairwell. Long way up to 350—taking the elevator to 349 was a minor temptation, but there was no way to know if one of Noah's soldiers was monitoring the elevators.

So he spot-traveled a landing at a time, all the way up.

⚜⚜⚜

Standing at the stairwell door, Daniel struggled to make sense of all the emotions flooding in. At least a dozen people nearby, radiating manic euphoria, raging anger, confusion, loneliness, despair . . .

Daniel opened the door an inch and peered through the gap to see a brightly lit hallway, eight feet wide, solid steel doors evenly spaced along both sides of the hall. Each door had a small rectangular window, and beside each door handle was an electronic security card reader.

Daniel could hear no footsteps or voices in the area.

He stepped into the hallway and eased the door closed behind him, moved to the first door on his right and put his face to the window.

Jesus.

Thick padding covered every inch of the small room's walls and floor. No bed, no toilet, no sink. Sitting on the floor, facing away from the door, a middle-aged woman in a heavy canvas straitjacket with thick leather straps, her pale head shaved, rocked forward and back, forward and back, forward and back . . .

This was a mental ward for those who got lost.

Daniel crept to the next cell, where a young man struggled against his straitjacket, his face contorted with rage. Yelling something, but the rooms were completely soundproofed and Daniel couldn't read his lips.

And then Daniel heard his name.

22

Daniel wasn't hearing with his ears, but in his mind's ear. Still, he knew it originated from the last door on his left. He had no idea *how* he knew, but he knew it with certainty just the same.

A quick glance back to the stairwell, listening hard. All clear. He approached the door, focusing his attention on the emotion radiating from within. A sickening, howling terror, fight-or-flight response short-circuiting, resulting in frozen panic.

Daniel Byrne—Daniel—Daniel Byrne . . .

He forced himself to the window, coming face-to-face with the man just a few inches away on the other side. The man did not struggle against his straitjacket, but stood locked in place, body trembling, jaw clenched, breath shallow and strained, tendons popping in his neck and veins in his temple, face crimsoned and eyes bloodshot from the strain.

Daniel Byrne—Daniel—Daniel Byrne . . .

The man was repeating Daniel's name like a mantra; it was not an attempt to communicate, and he stared right through Daniel, not seeing him at all.

Was this man one of the disappeared agitators Digger had talked about? And was he also Jay Eckinsburger, the Foundation field op who said Daniel Byrne was coming, and who was currently sedated in a five-star asylum on Earth? Could the consciousness bifurcate? Could a person be conscious in both Source and Earth at the same time?

Was that what snapped this man's mind?

Whoever the man was, if this were happening on Earth, he would be dead inside a month. The human body simply can't stay continually maxed out on adrenaline without breaking down. Most likely, the man would suffer a stroke or cardiac arrest, but the real cause of death would be unrelenting panic. Did it work the same way here? Regardless, the man was in desperate need of relief, and Noah was not having him sedated.

This was not a mental ward.

This was hell.

Summoning his will, Daniel kept his speed in check and his footfalls soft as he retreated to the stairwell, blocking out the emotional frenzy of the lost souls locked behind steel doors.

He spot-traveled up to the next landing, and the next, and the next, as fast as he could. How many floors of hell before all the lost had been straitjacketed and stored, locked and padded cells replaced by living quarters? Daniel didn't slow down to find out. He focused his attention ahead, away from the madness, spot-traveling landing to landing, not stopping until he reached the top floor.

This was the floor where Digger had said they meditated, where Noah gave his sermons. Standing against the stairwell door, Daniel focused his attention on the other side.

But he felt no presence on the other side of the door. Nothing at all. He cracked the door open an inch and drew a breath.

The place was packed, more than a thousand people meditating together, not sitting lotus or zazen, just sitting, with perfect posture, on little red chairs, upturned hands resting on knees, sitting in rows that spanned the entire floor, wall to wall—no windows to provide a view that might distract. Every age and ethnic origin seemed accounted for. People plucked at random from every corner of the world. Like AIT, this *crossing over*—or *waking up*—whatever it was, it did not discriminate.

Everyone wore the same outfit. Black pants and red shirt, cut for comfort, like you might encounter at an exclusive Manhattan spa. Their meditative state was so deep that they did not notice as Daniel stepped inside and closed the door. Their eyes were open, all directed up at a bright light pouring down from what appeared to be a domed ceiling in the center of the meditation hall. The intensity of their concentration was unlike anything he'd ever seen, and the space above them seemed alive with energy.

Daniel forced a step forward while manifesting a pair of mirrored aviators in his pocket. He put them on and looked up. Even with sunglasses, he had to squint.

A holographic image—more solid looking than current technology on Earth could create—hung directly above the meditators, suspended in the light. Three-dimensional, stretching maybe thirty feet in each direction.

It looked like the interior of an old chapel. Tudor period, Daniel guessed. Dark wooden beams and colorful stained-glass windows. A large wooden cross on one wall. A suit of armor beneath a stained-glass window depicting Saint James the Apostle.

Portrait of the saint as a young man—alabaster skin, wavy blond hair hanging to his shoulders, wearing a red robe and a purple halo. Balanced on his left hand, an open book with a bright royal-blue cover.

Saint James held a large white feather quill, writing into the book. But he didn't look at the page as he wrote, his sinless gaze directed heavenward to better receive the word of God.

Daniel squinted deeper, above the hologram, into the light flooding in from the top of the dome. This light was not glimmer, but it was more than just light. It *powered* the hologram, providing the meditators a common focus. It was sent for this purpose.

Sent by Noah.

The light pulsed, just barely, but Daniel spotted it.

Shit.

He sprinted for the stairs.

Bursting into the stairwell, Daniel spot-traveled down to the next landing and froze, the hair standing up on his forearms, his scalp electric.

He could feel the presence of Noah's soldiers closing in. Eight of them—hostile, driven, predators honing in on prey—three in the stairwell above, three below, and two now in the meditation hall, almost at the stairwell door.

Daniel spot-traveled down to the next level, yanked on the door handle, and burst into an empty white hallway, running blindly, feeling for a gap, a way between the predators.

He drew the pistol from his belt as the stairwell door behind him slammed open and two men ran into the hall, closing the distance.

Daniel squeezed off a round behind him, and as they ducked for cover he skidded left around a corner and ran down a hallway to the other stairwell.

Worse. Dozens of them here, surging into the stairwell above and below, now filling the hallway he'd just left, coming from everywhere, so many Daniel couldn't begin to keep track of them.

Footsteps echoed through the stairwell as Noah's soldiers closed in and even more joined the hunt. Daniel glanced at the pistol in his hand. It may as well have been a water pistol.

He aimed down the stairs and fired a round at nothing, just to buy a few precious seconds.

But there was no way out. Today would have to be a good day to die after all. And the dream of a future with Kara, either here or on Earth, would now die with him in this stairwell.

If you can see a place, you can be there.

But there were no windows in—

If you can see a place, you can be there.

Daniel drew a deep breath and closed his eyes.

✤ ✤ ✤

Breathe.

Daniel let out the breath he was holding and filled his lungs again. He was standing in the bedroom of his apartment in Source, just as he'd visualized, still holding the pistol. He'd spot-traveled miles from Noah's tower, to a place he could only see in his mind's eye.

"Holy crap," he said aloud.

Daniel sat on the edge of the bed and collected his thoughts. He returned the gun to the nightstand drawer, then walked through the living room to the apartment's front door.

Every time he'd tried to open the door on his early visits to Source, the vision (as he'd thought of it then) had ended and he'd returned home. During their dinner conversation, Digger had speculated that it wouldn't happen now that his whole consciousness was present in Source.

He turned the knob. The door opened.

Daniel shut the door and returned to the bedroom. He lay on his back on the bed, closed his eyes, and folded his hands across his chest.

I am sitting in a car.

In Belgium.

The air smells of coffee.

23
==

D aniel Byrne.
     Always Daniel Byrne, again and again. It was as if they were locked in perpetual battle, compelled by some absurd circular destiny.

This time it had to end.

Noah walked to the edge of the rooftop and looked straight into Primordial Reality.

The people called it glimmer.

The glimmer made them feel ill.

They couldn't even look at it.

They would never be able to look at it, because they would never be fully awake. Not even close. They'd never even be half-awake, most of their consciousness forever stuck in the dream of Earth. Which made them useful, if lesser, beings.

But Noah was fully awake.

And Noah loved the glimmer.

The glimmer didn't appear to Noah's eyes as a painfully bright light. To his eyes, it appeared as a vast kaleidoscope of fractals—shimmering and shifting, growing, expanding, shrinking, merging together and splitting apart, an infinitely complex dance of electric snowflakes.

It was, after all, the very stuff of creation.

Noah loved the glimmer so much, he'd completely surrounded his rooftop palace with glim. Standing here, there was no sky above, no seaside town below, no sunset in the distance. Just a dance of fractals, a womb of energy and potential, from which entire universes could be born.

If . . .

If Noah proved successful with the claim he'd been staking since he first awoke in Source. His claim to true godhood.

Not *if*, he corrected himself. Not *if*, but *when*.

And soon.

Noah stepped closer, right to the rooftop's edge. He held his right hand up, fingers spread wide, and watched as the skin on the back of his hand began to shimmer and shift in harmony with the dancing fractals, so close to such beautiful force, mere inches from the infinite.

He lowered his hand and stepped away from the glimmer, turning to face the elevators. It was cruel, of course, to summon Elias up here, to make him face the glimmer, but this was the man's third consecutive failure, so a little pain was in order.

The first failure in the alley was forgivable, really. While Digger's disdain for Noah had been plain to feel, Elias had warned all the stragglers away from Daniel and had visited Digger in the dream to warn her a second time. That should've been enough. Elias couldn't have foreseen her risking her life to help Daniel, in the face of Noah's power. She'd made an unnatural choice.

The failure in the dream—in Barbados—however, was less forgivable, and there simply could be no excuse for this latest.

And all the while, Daniel was becoming—and would continue to become—more awake. And more powerful. He'd been in the bloody meditation hall—*one floor down*—before Noah even felt his presence. He'd spot-traveled from a windowless stairwell. And after crossing back into the dream, he'd completely vanished. However hard Noah tried—and he'd focused his entire mind on it—he could no longer see Daniel Byrne in the dream.

Damn it to hell.

Noah caught himself and snorted a sharp laugh.

A simple shift of perspective was all he needed. There was actually some satisfaction to take from the fact that it would be Daniel Byrne's resistance that would provide the test to Noah's claim to godhood. From the perspective of a god, Daniel was not an enemy, but a mechanism for advancement—a stepping stone leading to where Noah deserved to be.

Even before Noah had awakened, even when he'd been locked in the dream, he'd always burned with the desire to become more. To not only serve God, but to partner with him.

And once he awoke, he'd learned how close he was.

Noah thought back to the moment his Earth dream ended—the moment of his awakening in Source. He remembered it often. He considered it the moment of his true birth.

A birth in blood—his own blood—yet he was born here undamaged. Born powerful beyond imagining. The only being in Source who stood completely outside the dream.

Only Noah could look directly into the glimmer and see that it was the source of the dream, and only he could bend the glimmer to his will.

While the lesser, half-awake beings marveled at their ability to manifest insignificant baubles, Noah had built a magnificent tower topped by a glimmer womb. And then he'd explored his power further, giving the glimmer his full attention, and he realized he could make . . . anything.

He supposed this was how the dream of Earth began. Perhaps some other god before Noah had set it in motion and left it for Noah to make perfect.

Daniel Byrne was the last obstacle. Daniel was becoming more awake with each visit and had already exhibited power far beyond the others. Could he become fully awake? Like Noah? That very risk was why Noah had forbidden Elias to kill Daniel in the dream. What if he woke up here with greater power?

But time was running short. The dance with Daniel Byrne had to end.

The elevator chimed and the doors slid open. Noah waited.

After a few long seconds, Elias emerged, forcing his legs into halting steps, fear radiating out in front of him, eyes hidden behind sunglasses, hands forming a visor against his forehead in a desperate attempt to shield himself from the glimmer. He managed four steps out onto the rooftop before falling to his knees, as if the glimmer were pressing him down. His stomach heaved twice. The third time, he vomited.

Noah watched until Elias had completely emptied his stomach.

"Had enough?"

Elias jerked a nod. "Please, Lord. Mercy."

"Oh, all right." Noah manifested plain white walls and a ceiling, temporarily sacrificing the beautiful fractal dance.

Elias wiped his mouth with his sleeve as he got to his feet. With ill-disguised trepidation, he removed the sunglasses. He said, "I know I let you down, Lord—"

"'Sir' will do nicely," said Noah, "when we're alone."

"Yes, sir," said Elias, clearly honored by the privilege just awarded him, but confused by the close proximity of pain and kindness.

Noah said, "You did let me down. Did I not warn you in advance?"

"Yes, sir, you did."

"I told you not to underestimate him."

"Yes." Elias winced. "But he did something nobody else can do. I mean, nobody but you."

"Don't make excuses, Elias. It's tiresome. Your mission in life is to remove nuisances from my sight. Daniel Byrne is a nuisance, and the longer he continues, the more tenuous your value to me becomes. That's not too difficult a concept for you, is it?"

"No, sir."

"Good. Because I am done making allowances for failure." Noah softened his tone slightly to shift the man's focus to the task at hand. "Clearly Daniel possesses abilities, when awake, that you do not. So I'm rescinding my earlier edict. You may now kill him in the dream, where you're on equal footing."

Profound relief radiated out from Elias. "Thank you, sir. I'll go right now. Where in the dream can I find him?"

Noah waved that away. Bad enough that Daniel was performing magic tricks of his own to awe the natives; no way would Noah admit he couldn't even find Daniel in the dream anymore.

"I have something else in mind," he said. "Instead of sending you to Daniel, this time I'll arrange for him to come to you."

24

Daniel awoke in a bed, but not his bed in Source. That bed had a hard mattress and a wool blanket. Daniel now lay in a soft bed, under a down duvet.

This presented a problem, because Daniel couldn't remember how he got here, and he had no idea where *here* was. The last thing he remembered before waking was folding his hands across his chest, lying atop the wool blanket in Source, with the intention of returning to the car in Belgium.

He spent another minute with his eyes closed, trying to remember, but nothing came. He opened his eyes and looked to his right.

A modern, elegantly appointed hotel room, cast in the warm light of silk-shaded lamps. He couldn't see any detail outside the window—the sheers were drawn—but he could see that it was nighttime.

While the hotel room was unfamiliar, everything looked normal enough. But something wasn't right; something about the room didn't quite feel real. Daniel felt as if he were asleep—like waking up in this room had been the start of a dream that began with waking up in this room.

That way lies madness.

He pushed himself up to sitting. Digger had taught him that sensory input smoothed the transition of crossing over, so he began pleating the bedsheet between his fingers. But the signals his brain now received from the nerve endings of his fingers felt . . .

Muted.

Because now you've felt the real thing in Source.

Because Earth is just a dream.

Daniel slammed a fist into the pillow beside him. "Shit," he said aloud. "I don't know what's real anymore."

"Who does, brother? Who the hell does?"

Daniel swiveled his head to see Pat sitting in an armchair to his left. Pat closed the Rebus novel he'd been reading and gave Daniel a serious nod that said: *Take it easy.*

"Where the hell am I?"

"*We*," said Pat. "*We* are in the Hotel Amigo, in beautiful downtown Brussels." He put the book aside and leaned forward, elbows propped on his knees. "When you came to—"

"In the car."

"Yes, in the car. You—"

"I have no memory of it."

"Yeah," said Pat, "so shut up for a second and let me finish a sentence."

"Right, sorry. Go."

"When you came to—in the car—you were really weird." Pat shrugged, conceding the obvious. "I mean, weirder than you are now. You were having some kind of episode—manic, babbling nonsense. Some of it wasn't even English, sounded kinda like Tim used to, when a fit hit him, like speakin' in tongues."

Daniel remembered driving into New Orleans, his uncle beside him in the passenger seat, when Tim was rocked by a particularly violent fit—not the phony speaking-in-tongues performance of his televangelist act, but the real deal, courtesy of AIT. The memory made him shudder.

"Damn."

"Yeah. At first I thought, you know, *dissociative state*, but you came to on your own—I didn't wake you up."

Daniel opened his mouth to speak, then closed it.

"What?" said Pat.

"I was thinking: Of course you didn't wake me up. I was awake when I was in Source." He looked around the room. "I don't even know what this place is. I—I don't feel awake."

Pat made a calming gesture with both hands. "Dude. Freak out a little quieter or you'll wake the neighbors." He stood and crossed to the desk and filled a mug with coffee from a thermal carafe. "Anyway, it wasn't a dissociative state—you knew who we both were, and where we were. You kept insisting Noah couldn't find you now. Things had changed, you said."

"It's true," said Daniel. "I got right up in his kitchen and he didn't feel my presence until I put my attention on the energy he was sending down."

"I'm just gonna assume that makes sense to one of us," said Pat.

"Basically, he noticed me noticing him. Not before."

"Ditto," said Pat. "Sugar?"

"No thanks."

"Maybe it was a trap." Pat carried the mug to the bed. "Maybe Noah laid out the red carpet for you, just pretending not to notice until you got close. Maybe he wanted to capture you."

Daniel took the mug with a nod. "No. When the light dipped, I could feel his shock and anger. He didn't know. And his goons didn't aim to capture, they came after me with murderous intent. You can feel people's emotions from a distance in Source."

"Okay, so something's changed and now Noah can't see you from afar, so long as you don't put your attention on him."

"Right. Which gives me an idea." Daniel sipped some coffee. It tasted weak, thin, not much like coffee at all. He took a larger swallow, then gulped down the rest.

Nothing.

Daniel sailed the mug across the room, where it bounced off the wall and broke against the edge of a table.

Pat followed the fate of the mug, then looked back to Daniel and raised his eyebrows.

Daniel said, "We're in a five-star hotel in Belgium. I can assume the coffee's pretty good, right?"

"The fuck, man?" Pat snorted out a bemused laugh, without humor. "The coffee ain't up to your standards? Seriously?"

"No, you don't understand. I'm asking you. Is the coffee good?"

"What? Yes, the coffee's good."

"Strong."

"Yes, Daniel. The coffee is strong."

"Tastes like brown water to me."

Pat poured a mug for himself, took a sip. "It's just coffee, man. Look, I know it's easy for me to say, but I don't think the professor sacrificed her life so you could climb up your own ass." He sipped some more coffee. "And I mean that with love."

Daniel nodded, got out of bed. "Yeah, you're right. I'm just having a bumpy landing. Need to reboot." He headed toward the bathroom. "I'm gonna hop in the shower. Do me a favor, order us up some room service. I'm starving."

25

Daniel could barely taste the grilled octopus, but his body needed the protein, so he ate it all, while telling Pat about his increasing power in Source, about meeting Huck and spot-traveling long distances and manifesting dumpsters, and everything he'd seen and done in Noah's tower.

"Which brings us to my idea," he said, depositing his empty plate on the room-service trolley. "We don't know who the hell Noah even is on Earth. He could be anyone."

"Tell you what," said Pat. "He could be runnin' for president or prime minister someplace, got a 6-6-6 birthmark on his scalp. Or maybe he already won." He whistled an impression of a theremin.

It made Daniel laugh, and he started to feel like he wasn't dreaming after all. He said, "Or he could be some war vet with a traumatic brain injury, sleeping rough, living under bridges with his dog. No way to know. But we know Elias—"

He stopped short. Thinking of these people by their Source names was not helping Earth feel like less of a dream. Digger had been a woman living on Earth, an archeologist from New England working as a professor in Spain, and her name was Dana Cameron.

Huck was a sad boy named George from Kokomo, Indiana, who bounced around foster homes.

Real people, living real lives.

"We know Lucien Drapeau," he said. "Whatever Drapeau's got cookin' on Earth is in service to Noah's agenda. You can take that to the bank. So we fly to New York, get my Drapeau file from Vasili's locker, and we go through his known associates, find him that way. Keeping my focus on Elias—Drapeau—instead of Noah."

"And Noah won't be able to see you, 'cause your attention ain't on him." Pat grinned. "Sounds like a plan."

Daniel sat at the desk and woke the laptop computer. He scanned his thumbprint on the laptop's pad and brought a secure web browser up on the screen.

Pat said, "Use the UK passports, they're still clean."

"In a minute," said Daniel, as he typed his current password to access his voice-mail. "First, you know the best part of my go-to-New-York plan?"

Pat said, "You're taking me ice-skating at Rockefeller Center."

"Better." Daniel swiveled his chair to face Pat directly. "Kara. And me. In New York, with twinkly Christmas lights, not ice-skating 'cause I'd fall on my ass, but dinner, wine, maybe a piano bar. I'm gonna send her a ticket."

"That does sound lovely, and I hate to be the voice of reason, but you think it's wise to take your eye off the ball right now for a romantic rendezvous with the girlfriend? Come on, man, you're smarter than that. Get your head in the game."

"This coming from a guy who's never kept a girlfriend longer than six months."

"It's not relationship advice, idiot. It's survival advice."

"It's not up for debate. I need to see her. I need to look into her eyes and hear what she has to say, and I need to show her that, my recent behavior to the contrary, I want her in my life."

"Oh, gag me with a pitchfork," said Pat, pulling a pack of Dunhills from his pocket. He shook a cigarette from the pack. "I'm gonna step out on the roof. Be sure to let me know when you're done ovulatin."

Daniel shot Pat a friendly middle finger as Pat opened the window and climbed outside. Clicking through to his inbox, Daniel found a new voice-mail from Kara. A long one. He brought the transcript up on the screen.

> Got your email. Whatever you're doing, whatever's occupying your time, it's clearly the most important thing in your life right now—but since I don't know what it is, I don't know what that means. But I have a decision to make that won't wait until you can fit me into your schedule. And you can remove the sarcasm from that last statement if you're being chased by armed bad guys or something. I hope you're safe, even if I sorta want to kill you myself. I hate that you've put me in this position and I didn't want to tell you this way, but you've given me no choice.

I'm pregnant. And unless the archangel Michael paid me a visit in my sleep, you're the father.

I'm angry I can't see your face right now. Angry I'm going to get back a considered response instead of the raw truth of how you feel about this. Truth is, we don't know each other that well, not really. There hasn't been time. I don't even know if being a father is something you see for yourself.

I'm keeping my baby—you don't get a vote in that. You do get to decide if you want to be involved with raising your child. As for you and me . . . I have no idea.

I'm in San Diego this week. Interviewed at the UCSD Medical Center, and it went well. I expect they're going to offer me the job. I just . . . I thought we should discuss it first but . . . I don't know. Talking to an answering machine sucks. This isn't fair to me.

I don't know what else to say. I'm staying at the Marriott Marquis. Room 2309. Come see me, or don't.

The ball's in your court.

Daniel sat motionless for a few seconds, reflexively doing the math in his head. The night the condom broke. They'd laughed about it at the time, sweat-soaked bodies collapsing together. They'd been drinking champagne. Kara would be four months, maybe four and a half. So, an April baby, or maybe late March. Springtime. Renewal.

He stood and snatched the laptop from the desk, strode into the bathroom, and closed the door behind him. He set the laptop down on the marble countertop.

Then he clicked Record Message.

"Listen, you: No risk of a considered response; it's been all of thirty seconds since I read your voice-mail. What follows is exactly the truth of how I feel about this.

"I feel like the luckiest guy in the world. Also a bit scared to be honest, but having a kid is a big step, so that's normal. Mostly, I can't wait to see you and get started on this journey. And I want to be more than involved, I want us to raise our child together. I want to be there for the pregnancy, the birth, changing diapers, first day of school, teenage tantrums—I want to be there for all of it. What I'm saying is: I'm in.

"You say we don't know each other that well, but I think that's fear talking. We haven't been together that long, but what we've been through together . . . I think we do know each other. And, lady, I swear we are for each other."

Daniel reached for the trackpad to hit Send. Instead, he played it back, to hear how it would sound to Kara.

He clicked Erase Message.

Then he hit Record Message again.

"I'm on my way," he said.

He hit Send.

26

From the hotel rooftop, Brussels was a perfect picture postcard: magnificent gothic architecture, towering spires illuminated by floodlights, a crescent moon hanging high above.

Pat blew a plume of smoke into the night sky. "You skip school the day they taught birth control in health class?"

Daniel shrugged. "You know how it says on the box, *98 percent effective*?"

"Well, shit," said Pat.

"I think you just mispronounced *congratulations*," said Daniel.

"You can't seriously want to bring a child into this world, not after all you've seen."

"I think I liked you better when you were a pothead," said Daniel. "This cynicism pose is getting out of hand."

"Ain't posin'," said Pat. "You think I sold my house and gave away my dog and moved to a boat on a lark?"

"You gave Edgar away?"

"I found him a good home," Pat said, a little defensively. Pat had once told Daniel that Edgar was the longest relationship of his adult life, with any living thing.

"You just walked away from him?"

Pat took a long drag on his cigarette and Daniel could see the pain in his eyes and wondered if he'd overstepped.

Pat said, "Look, man. World is going through a massive shift . . . dark days ahead. And they're almost upon us."

"Not if we can stop Noah."

"I ain't even talkin' about Noah, I'm talkin' about right here. I've been deeper in the belly of the beast than you, for a lot longer than you. I can see the patterns. History is cyclical, one step forward and three back, same shit in a different package, over and over. And right now, all the signs are aligned—the current empire is about to fall, and we're past the tipping point. The plutocrats know it, and they're doing what they always do—same thing they did at the end of Rome and every other empire. They're asset stripping, funneling wealth to the top and selling war to the masses, everything on credit, bankrupting the dying empire even faster. And the rate of their asset stripping tells us we're past the tipping point, because they're no longer shearin' the sheep. They're skinnin' the sheep."

"You are just a ray of sunshine," said Daniel.

"Tough titties," said Pat. "I'm telling you this so you can start thinking about gettin' ready, 'cause the shitstorm's coming, like it or not. Planet's getting hotter, less arable land, pretty soon we gonna have water refugees on our doorstep, and we're still burning dead dinosaurs to run our machines. There's gonna be a disease pandemic in the next century 'cause we destroyed antibiotics with our greed and desire for constant comfort. And look at what our governments focus on—look at the villains and con artists running for high office. And winning. They ain't runnin' as public servants, they're runnin' as saviors. And one thing has always been true—every time people think they're voting for a savior, they end up electing a tyrant.

"Not to put too fine a point on it, but so-called 'Western democracy' is dying of corruption, and authoritarianism is on the rise again, and it's a worldwide thing. The social order's under stress, and now people are realizing AIT is spreading faster than anyone in charge of anything is admitting, and the protests are growing faster than Occupy, faster than anything. The Foundation expects mass violence will paralyze London during the G7 next month—I'm tellin' you, the whole house of cards could come tumbling down even sooner than I think."

"And your solution is to not have children?"

"Be a start," said Pat. "Everybody had just one kid for the next three generations, our great-grandchildren would be born into a world of plenty. Enough for everyone."

"Make you a deal," said Daniel. "I stick to just one, and you find a way to be happy for me."

Pat put on a game-show-host smile, toasted Daniel with his cigarette. "Congratulations, I'm sure you'll make a swell dad."

"Thank you." Daniel looked across the city to the spire atop the Hôtel de Ville, where a gilded Saint Michael, wings rising behind his shoulders in triumph, impaled Lucifer during the battle for heaven. Michael the archangel, who would later visit Mary with the news of her miraculous pregnancy.

Funny that Kara had made reference to the archangel in her voice-mail message. Felt like the kind of synchronicity that happens in dreams. But Kara was real and the baby growing inside her was real and Daniel, ready or not, was really going to be a dad.

Would he be a good one? Hard to say. Daniel's mother had died in childbirth and his father had committed suicide three hours later by throwing himself off the Greater New Orleans Bridge. So he'd been raised by his uncle, a world-class con artist.

Consequently, he had to admit, his reference point for fatherhood was perhaps less than ideal. As a role model, Trinity had left almost everything to be desired, and Daniel hadn't made it through childhood undamaged, but who really does? Despite his shortcomings, Trinity had loved Daniel and treated him with kindness.

That was a start.

Daniel said, "Remember that Bible Tim carried everywhere and waved around on television all the time? Bright royal-blue cover?"

"Whole world does," said Pat. "Hell, they sell Tim Trinity editions now. Pages edged in silver, blue leather cover, just like Tim's."

Daniel nodded. "In Noah's tower, in the meditation hall, there was kind of a hologram of the shared meditation—"

"You told me. Tudor chapel."

"Right. In the chapel, there was a stained-glass portrait of Saint James the Apostle. He was writing with a quill, writing his letter in a royal-blue Bible, just like Tim's."

"Huh," said Pat.

"Feels like a clue," said Daniel.

"But to what?"

Daniel thought about it. "Remember Tim's last television broadcast, before we went on the run?"

"Shortest sermon in history," said Pat.

"Exactly. He quoted Saint James—said faith without works is dead. And then he had some kind of panic attack and bolted off the stage. The media hyped the hell out of it." Daniel remembered how the cable news announcers had immediately dubbed it Trinity's Faith Without Works Is Dead sermon, which seemed a little on the nose, since that's basically all he'd said.

"I remember the controversy," said Pat. "Tim didn't just say Saint James was right, he said Saint Paul was wrong. He basically said faith don't matter a lick, and *only* works matter. Why they killed him, if you ask me."

"The hell are you talking about?" said Daniel. "Conrad Winter had Tim killed to prevent the world from learning about the existence of AIT, because the Council was working to harness it for themselves. We know this."

Pat lit a new cigarette with the dying butt of the last. He said, "Sure, but people often have multiple motivations. What I'm saying: Tim had the whole world watching, and what did he say? He said that to love each other as brothers and sisters means to *treat* each other as brothers and sisters. You know who else came carrying that message? Robert F. Kennedy, Martin Luther King, Gandhi, Jesus, to name but a few . . . all carried that message, all had followings that grew uncomfortably large for the power brokers of the day, all assassinated. Tim, too. And you can add Bob Marley to the list, except the guys they hired botched the job."

"And by 'they,' you mean 'they' the plutocrats? You think a secret cabal of plutocrats conspired to assassinate Bob Marley?"

"Well, *duh*," said Pat. "Don't you read history?"

"How do you square this world view with working for the Foundation?" said Daniel.

"It's like what Jacob said in Liberia: There are no good guys in this game. There's only bad guys, and *less bad* guys. I work with Carter Ames because he's one of the less bad guys."

"Why play the game at all?" said Daniel.

Anger flashed in Pat's eyes. "Because, Mr. No More Collateral Damage, the game will be played with or without me, and somebody's gonna win. Foundation sure as hell ain't pure, but those authoritarian movements on the rise? They're financed by the Council. Billions of dollars, dark money shifted 'round the globe, funneled to ultra-nationalists, fanatical religious groups, terrorist cells, you name it. And Conrad Winter's parting gift to the world? He's pushed the Middle East from *manageable instability* to utter chaos. Yemen, Syria, it's all falling apart."

Pat took one last hit off the cigarette, ground it under a heel, and looked square at Daniel. "I told you not to join the game. I told you you wouldn't like what you learned. But now that you know, how can you sit on the sidelines?"

Dana Cameron's warning flashed in Daniel's mind. A devastated city, more than a thousand people dead, caused by him. He still had no idea where, or when, or how he would cause it, or how to stop it.

He said, "I just don't want any more blood on my hands."

Pat said, "You play the game right, you hurt some people, you get blood on your hands for true, but you help more people. Like Carter always says, it's the math of the thing. But you don't play the game at all, even more people get hurt because you wanna pretend you don't know what you know so you can go on enjoying your privileged life. That don't seem so morally pure to me."

They stood on the rooftop in silence for a minute.

Then Daniel said, "Full marks for honesty, I'll give you that."

Pat's expression softened. "You're my brother and I love you, whatever you do. Hell, I'll even come to San Diego—which, for the record, is maybe the dumbest decision you've ever made—just to watch your back. Noah may not be able to see you, but every time we pass through an airport, every time we rent a car, we're on camera. And Drapeau can tap into the surveillance web just like the Foundation can. We could use the Foundation's resources, and the grudge you're holding against Carter ain't helping."

Daniel nodded. "I'll think about it. Meanwhile, we won't be flying into California. I booked us to Las Vegas. We'll pick up guns there and drive to San Diego."

"That's clever," said Pat. "Just the kind of clever that'll get you killed one of these days."

Daniel said, "Even if I went to Carter for help, how do you think that would play? I tell him Lucien Drapeau serves a malevolent demigod named Noah who rules a universe called Source, where people can spot-travel and manifest shit out of pure intention—a universe that's fundamental to ours, maybe even creates ours. In fact, Source may be the *only* reality and Earth is just a dream we're having. He'd have me locked up with Jay Eckinsburger."

"Nah, he wouldn't. Look, your uncle thought God was talkin' to him, right? That Blankenship kid in West Virginia thought he was possessed by Satan. Your baby-mama thought the CIA was beaming voices into her head with microwaves or whatever. They were all wrong; it was just their way of giving context to the flood of information from AIT. So Carter would take it as that, and try to tease out whatever it is AIT is telling you."

Daniel looked back to the gilded Saint Michael vanquishing Lucifer, after Lucifer decided he would no longer submit to the authority of God and tried to topple God from his throne.

The work of men who strive to become gods.

It was something the voice in Kara's head had said when they were in Norway. At the time, it described the work the Council was doing in Liberia and South Carolina—creating a designer plague, trying to harness the power of AIT and use it for themselves. But didn't it apply to Noah as well, trying to reshape Source in his own image and tolerating no dissent?

Daniel looked at Pat, said, "Is that what you think? That these trips to Source are just my brain's way of giving context to AIT?"

Pat said, "I already told you. I actually think we *are* livin' in a dream, just not a good one. Maybe Source is real, maybe not. But maybe Earth ain't real, either. And what difference does it make? Like you said, brother, we all gotta surf the wave."

27

San Diego's waterfront sparkled under the midday sun. Daniel and Pat walked along the jetty outside the Marriott Marquis, pleasure boats lining docks in the marina to their left, the Pacific Ocean beyond. The place was alive with color and movement. Tourists with selfie sticks posing before palm trees, couples canoodling on park benches, tattooed dog walkers walking designer dogs, a septuagenarian hippie on roller skates skating lazy figure eights along the pier.

Pat shot a look at the yellow roses clutched in Daniel's hand. He said, "After you take out Drapeau and fix Noah's wagon, you gonna be a doctor's husband in San Diego?"

"Could do," said Daniel. "I hear there are sometimes job openings for doctors in Barbados, too."

"Dream big, my brother," said Pat with a wide grin.

As they crossed the park to the hotel entrance, Pat pulled a pack of gum from his pocket. "Not cinnamon, I promise. Minty fresh."

Daniel popped a piece from the pack. "Thanks."

The lobby was all modern air-conditioned luxury. Daniel and Pat walked through the reception area and past the open bar, navigating around business travelers and well-heeled tourists.

Pat said, "You seem a little nervous," as they reached the elevators.

Daniel pressed the Up button. "I'm about to see the pregnant mother of my child and ask her to consider the possibility that we might raise that child together, maybe even spend the rest of our lives together. And then I'm gonna say, 'But I can't really hang around right now, because Bad Guys, so we'll have to continue this conversation by voice-mail until I get shit sorted.' How do you like my chances?"

"Dude, you brought roses. Chicks dig that shit. 'Course, they shoulda been red, but—"

"Wait," said Daniel.

"I'm kidding. The flowers are fine."

"No, something about this place is wrong." Daniel looked past Pat, across the hall and into the open bar, and immediately saw what was wrong. "Guy at the end of the bar, red curly hair. Looks like a guy I saw in a photo with Drapeau—café in Barcelona."

"*Looks like*, or—?"

"I'm not sure." Daniel's peripheral vision told him the redheaded man was now looking in their direction. "He's looking." The man stood quickly from his barstool and strode away, just shy of breaking into a jog. "He's making tracks." Behind Daniel, the elevator door opened.

Pat said, "I'm on him. You get Kara," and headed after the man.

Daniel stepped into the elevator. A man in a suit started to get on with him. Daniel put his hand over his mouth, looked at the man, and said, "I think I'm gonna be sick."

"I'll get the next one." The man backed out and the doors closed. Daniel tossed the flowers, pulled the pistol from his belt.

The ride up gave him time to wonder if he'd overreacted. Millions of men have curly red hair, and it was the hair that had caught Daniel's eye. He compared his memory of the man in the photo to his more recent memory of the man downstairs. Size and build were similar, but also average. Both had pale complexions, as do most people with that shade of hair. The photo had been taken from a different angle and the man had worn mirrored sunglasses, so comparing facial features was difficult. Not a lot else to go on. The man downstairs could very well just be a random redhead with a sudden attack of the trots, in a hurry to get to the men's room.

And a pistol was decidedly less romantic than roses.

Daniel glanced down at the flowers on the elevator floor, but he didn't pick them up. The elevator pinged and the doors opened and a gloved fist slammed into Daniel's mouth.

A lead-filled leather sap glove, and the blow landed with professional force, snapping Daniel's head back and splitting his lip. The world went dark for a second, while a kettledrum echoed around his skull. He felt himself stumble back but stayed on his feet. His vision returned blotchy and he pivoted to fire, but Lucien Drapeau was fast with his feet and kicked the gun from Daniel's hand.

The doors closed and the elevator started down and Daniel's vision was still blurred, but now training and the will to survive took over. He managed to get hold of a wrist as a blade swung into view and he turned into Drapeau, pivoting, guiding him into orbit, locking the wrist past the point where it was designed to bend so the knife clattered to the floor. But Drapeau knew how to counter, pivoted, broke the wrist lock, and introduced a knee into Daniel's kidney and a hammer fist to the neck that Daniel almost avoided.

Daniel bounced off the back wall and the doors opened and Drapeau grabbed his arm and hauled, sending Daniel sprawling to the floor of the hotel lobby. People screamed and the elevator doors closed, taking Daniel's gun.

But instead of renewing his attack, Drapeau turned and ran, pin-balling off several hotel guests on his way out the door.

Daniel scrambled to his feet, spat blood on the floor, and gave chase, determined not to lose sight of the assassin. He had no doubt Pat would take care of the redheaded man.

Drapeau sprinted through the little park, hurdled a bench, and turned north along the jetty. Daniel should've been slower—he'd sustained more damage in the fight—but rage was a powerful drug and this man had come after Kara and the baby growing inside her, and Daniel steadily closed the distance between them as the chase continued along the wharf, away from the hotel.

Drapeau ran down a pier that jutted out from land and dead-ended twenty yards from shore. No other people on the pier. He hadn't really been trying to get away, Daniel realized. He knew Daniel had sustained more damage, and neither had a weapon now, and he'd drawn Daniel here, away from the crowd.

It didn't matter.

Daniel followed, entering the pier and slowing to a brisk walk, just as Drapeau reached the end. Drapeau stopped and turned to face Daniel.

Daniel kept walking.

Drapeau took off his jacket, draped it over a railing.

Daniel kept walking.

The assassin spread his arms to encompass the wide world. He said, "You know, all this? It's just a dream. You're about to die trying to protect a dream."

Daniel kept walking.

Drapeau took a fighter's stance, inviting Daniel's approach. He said, "At least you're gonna die in your sleep. Isn't that what most people want, after all?"

Daniel lunged and the other man sidestepped and kicked at his knee, but Daniel slipped it, got inside, and drove an elbow at the man's sternum. Drapeau stepped back and regained his balance, then launched a kick that Daniel managed to parry. Then a hammer fist that made glancing contact with Daniel's cheek.

Drapeau was very good, but Daniel was good and angry, and got in a solid counterpunch before Drapeau pivoted and went for a throw. Daniel managed to grab fistfuls of the man's shirt and went with the momentum. Both men tumbled off the pier and splashed into the ocean.

The world became tiny swirling bubbles and salt water, the two men clawing and scratching just below the surface, kicking against the weight of sodden clothes and shoes, kicking at each other, but Drapeau had the advantage, and he grabbed a handful of Daniel's hair and pushed him down, and the world dimmed but Daniel hung on, because if he was gonna die, this asshole was sure as hell gonna die with him.

Daniel's chest screamed for air and he fought against drawing water into his lungs, but he was slipping now, muscles starved of oxygen, losing strength, and—no more *if*—he knew he was going to die.

The memory of being waterboarded in a hot cinderblock room in Monrovia flooded his mind, and then he remembered Kara's joy at seeing him alive and he knew they could've had a happy life together if only Dana Cameron had been able to teach him enough to beat Noah, but Cameron was dead and now Daniel would die and Cameron was Digger and Digger had worn a T-shirt and the T-shirt had said—

Wake Up!

✠ ✠ ✠

Daniel broke the surface, gulping air. He turned toward the shore to see Elias crawling up onto the beach and kneeling on the sand, coughing up water, the seaside town rising behind, white stucco and terra-cotta roofs bathed in golden, *magic hour* sunlight.

Daniel stared up at Noah's tower in the distance. He'd done it. He'd dragged them across to Source.

The surf was calm, and Daniel was close enough to stand and wade the rest of the way in, hitting shore as Elias struggled to his feet and began backing away from him, stammering.

"You—you—you . . ."

"I woke us up," said Daniel. "You should've left Kara alone."

"I didn't hurt her, I swear. She didn't even know I was in the hotel—I'm telling the truth. She's probably still in her room. You—you can go see her."

"Oh, I will. But you're never putting her in danger again." Daniel let the rage build inside him, and he knew Elias could feel it, too, just as Daniel could feel the fear growing in the other man. "And you're not gonna die in your sleep, Elias. You're gonna die wide-awake."

Daniel focused all his anger, bearing down on it, directing it to the very place where Elias stood, and the sand began to shimmer and shine, and the sound of thunder rose from below.

Elias held his hands out, palms forward. "No, no, Daniel, you don't want to do this—you can't—"

On pure will and fury, Daniel opened the earth under Elias's feet.

The beach cleaved in two and Elias slipped screaming into a black pit and sand poured in after him, the earth consuming him, until his screams turned to silence and the sand settled and was once more a beach.

When Daniel tried to draw a breath, it caught in his throat. Salt water rose from his lungs and erupted from his mouth, splashing onto the sand, and he remembered he was drowning under a pier in San Diego.

He closed his eyes and thought back to the water.

28

Daniel let out the breath he was holding and filled his lungs again. He opened his eyes. He was not in the water. He was lying on his back, looking up at the sky. Lying on the road.

Had someone hauled him out of the ocean?

He started to sit up but a stabbing pain in his side reminded him of the fight in the elevator, so he lay back and took inventory. He felt pretty beat up all over, and his left wrist was slightly sprained, but he decided nothing felt broken.

He could hear a siren, blocks away. Maybe whoever hauled him out of the water had called for an ambulance. Then he heard another siren, from the other direction, and another, and a helicopter above, and then the low horn of a fire engine, and now police sirens in the distance, and at least two more helicopters—

Daniel caught a flash-memory: just after he'd returned from Source, still in the water off the pier, still grasping handfuls of Drapeau's shirt, Drapeau floating dead in front of him. Daniel had let go and Drapeau had drifted down as Daniel kicked his legs and broke the surface, gulping air. And when he looked up, he saw a massive wall of water closing in, lifting him up . . .

He rose to sitting and looked down the street and tried to make sense of what he was seeing. Why was that car upside down? And the other turned over on its side? And palm trees lying across the street, and everything was wet, and power lines down, and windows smashed out of buildings—

He got to his feet and limped along the road, stunned, struggling to take it all in, navigating around felled trees and smashed cars and overturned newspaper boxes, broken glass crunching underfoot, sirens everywhere—

The sound of a baby crying—

The sound of a woman groaning in pain—

A man screaming—

Another man calling out—

"Harriet, for God's sake, where did you go? Harriet!"

People in shock, cradling broken arms, holding bloody faces, walking through the devastation, aimless, some in silent disbelief, others beyond hysterical.

Daniel couldn't process what he was seeing. He searched for the meaning of all this horror, but his mind was processing the input as a series of disjointed images without context and he felt disconnected, like he'd left a large chunk of his consciousness in Source.

He supposed he was in shock, too.

He kept on walking, trying to understand.

There were bodies. Some sprawled in the street, some lying against the sides of buildings.

Daniel stopped counting after ten.

Some of the walking wounded were not silent or hysterical, but spoke with hollow, expressionless voices, exchanging with passing strangers what few details they'd learned from emergency workers.

There'd been an extremely localized earthquake off the coast, generating a tsunami two stories high, a wall of water that slammed into the city. Over eight hundred already confirmed dead, tens of thousands as yet unaccounted for.

I am in blood . . .

Daniel stopped walking and tried to place the quote seeping up from memory. It seemed important.

I am in blood . . .

Shakespeare. It was from *Macbeth.*

I am in blood . . .

Daniel knew the play well, but he couldn't remember the next line. He told himself it would come if he stopped thinking about it. He walked in the direction of the nearest sirens. The sirens would lead him to the nearest hospital, and that's where he'd find Kara. She'd been far above the waterline; she would not have been injured. But she was a doctor, and in a public crisis she would do what good doctors do. She'd get to the nearest medical facility and lend a hand, just as she had in South Carolina.

It occurred to him that maybe he should get himself checked over for a concussion, since he was going to the hospital. He was still having trouble collecting his thoughts.

I am in blood . . . something.

Daniel hadn't passed anyone for a couple of blocks and there was a lull in the sirens. He wondered if he'd taken a wrong turn. He walked a bit farther, stopped, looked around.

He was alone on the block. And yet he felt . . .

He turned in the direction of the feeling, but there was no one there. Just the plain brick wall of a nondescript grocery store. He stepped closer, and the wall seemed to shimmer slightly, then became like a rippling, cloudy, liquid membrane, and Daniel could barely see through it, just enough to make out a man standing in a room with plain white walls. The membrane grew lighter, like some kind of aperture opening, like a—

Daniel realized he was looking through an impenetrable window into Source, and he knew the man on the other side was Noah.

Noah walked forward. Daniel stood rooted in place, unable to move, and the closer Noah got, the more familiar he looked, and then the membrane's haze lifted completely and Daniel could see right through.

He jerked back, feeling like the ground had just fallen out from under him, like the dream of falling that jerks you back from the edge of sleep.

"Hello, Daniel," said Conrad Winter.

29

C onrad . . . you're—dead."

Noah smiled. "I knew you'd be surprised. But not Conrad, no. Conrad Winter was just a dream I was having. And not dead. *Awake*, courtesy of your bullet. Fully alive, more alive than I ever could've imagined. The instant you shot me, the instant you saw me die, I was reborn in Source. Reborn a god." Noah touched his chest where Daniel had shot him. "I arrived with blood all over my shirt, two bullet holes in the fabric, right here. But no wound in my flesh. Proof that my life on Earth had been but a dream. I should thank you, really."

"You gonna thank me for killing Elias, too?"

Noah dismissed it with a wave. "I've got others. And you didn't kill me—you freed me."

"I might still kill you yet," said Daniel.

Noah laughed through his nose. "Interesting to see how many cities you'll destroy trying. Congratulations on San Diego, by the way."

Perhaps Daniel had been in shock, and maybe he had a concussion—or maybe he'd just been in denial. But now it all came clear. *He* had cleaved the earth in two under Elias. *He* had created the earthquake. All those bodies in the street, all the destruction, the lives destroyed. And Dana Cameron had seen it. She'd seen Daniel standing in the middle of a city he'd destroyed, and she'd tried to warn him.

He felt like throwing up.

"Really," said Noah. "Nice job. Everywhere you go, Daniel, corpses pile up. I know you don't approve of my methodology—even when I was dreaming you thought yourself superior—but the fact of the matter is, your body count now outstrips mine. Sure, I killed Stigmata Girl in Nigeria and your uncle, but you killed 269 with a drone strike. I killed a few hundred in Liberia, but you just snuffed out that many plus a thousand more in San Diego. Face it, every time you try to do good, you do bad. And yet you just keep on trying. At some point one has to wonder if maybe deep down you enjoy leaving bodies in your wake. Otherwise, you'd stop. You haven't the power to succeed, and yet you're perfectly willing to press on. It's curious, really." Noah shook his head, putting the subject aside. "I may not dream anymore, but I can still watch it. Whatever god before me created this dream—"

"Conrad, you're not a god."

"I seem to be. At any rate, I'm the only being here that stands outside the dream. And until some greater god shows up, I have the ability—and the responsibility—to make a better dream. Why would you even *want* to stop me?"

"It's not a dream," Daniel insisted. "These are real people. You were a real person once, too."

"That's just what you want to believe," said Noah. "But you've been to Source. You've been awake. Well, mostly awake. You know your power isn't close to mine and, frankly, even if it were, you're too late." He looked past Daniel to the ruined street. "Enjoy your handiwork, Daniel."

Noah turned and walked away, and the membrane clouded over and shimmered briefly, and Daniel was staring at a brick wall.

✤ ✤ ✤

I am in blood
Stepp'd in so far that, should I wade no more,
Returning were as tedious as go o'er.

✤ ✤ ✤

The lines from *Macbeth* rang in Daniel's ears as he trod down the center of the road, walking along the double yellow line. An ambulance passed and pulled to a stop beside a shirtless man sitting on the curb ahead. The man held a bunched-up T-shirt against the side of his head. Once white, the shirt was now completely sodden, dripping red. A triangle—Daniel looked closer—a seven-inch shard of glass jutted out from the man's shoulder, a stream of blood running down over a tattoo on his bicep.

A grinning skull, smoking a cigarette and wearing a top hat. A scroll beneath read:

Live Fast—Die Young

Daniel stood, turning around in place, taking it all in with clear eyes.

The dead, the wounded. The destruction.

Dream or not, an utter nightmare.

You caused this.

A woman's corpse lay against the side of a building, facedown, on top of a dead boy.

Daniel caught a flash-memory from Liberia—the woman and girl in the pit of bodies next to the Lofa River. And another—the bones of a long-dead family in a cave in Norway.

He forced himself to look at the corpses lying before him now, and to acknowledge what he saw. They'd been slammed against the side of the building by a wall of water. This was all his doing. He couldn't have been more responsible if he'd shot them both in the head.

Daniel threw up in the gutter.

30

The old television hanging above the bar was muted, thankfully. On the screen, images of the devastation in San Diego. A chyron text scroll at the bottom of the screen read:

SAN DIEGO QUAKE: 1,269 DEAD—6,000 INJURED

Daniel sat at a table, an ice bag on his left wrist, staring at the screen as it cut back to the anchor desk in the studio. The chyron now read:

IS CALIFORNIA READY FOR THE BIG ONE?

Across the bar, Pat hung up the payphone. He threaded his way between pool tables, took his seat across from Daniel, and drank from a bottle of root beer.

Pat said, "You were right. Miz Kara was at the hospital, doctorin'. My guys are all over it." He sipped from the bottle, added, "We're set, she's fine. And don't worry about Redhead—I was chasin' him through the parking lot when the tsunami hit. Dude got pancaked by a minivan."

Daniel adjusted the position of the ice bag on his wrist. "I know Conrad's unlikely to go after her again—she was just bait to get to me, and I think he's done talking to me—but I need to know she's safe. You sure of these guys?"

"San Diego is Navy SEAL City," said Pat. "My brothers. I got you the very best. Nobody's gonna mess with your girl."

Daniel nodded. "But I don't want her to know they're there—"

"Did I mention: SEALs? Unless and until they want to be seen, they're invisible."

"Okay," said Daniel. "Thank you."

"Anything for true love," said Pat.

They fell into an uneasy silence, sitting across from each other in the Hooz On First bar in Barstow, California, Pat sipping his root beer, Daniel drinking flavorless coffee and shifting the ice bag around his wrist, just to be doing something.

Daniel glanced up at the silent television over the bar. Scenes of a massive AIT protest in Chicago's Grant Park. The text scroll at the bottom of the screen read:

MENTAL HOSPITALS CROWDED
PATIENTS PREDICTING END TIMES
PROTESTORS DEMAND TRANSPARENCY

Pat broke the silence after a minute. "You really caused that earthquake, huh?"

"Yeah," said Daniel. "I really did."

"I'm sorry," said Pat.

"Me too."

"You couldn't have known what would happen. It was an accident."

"That's a cop-out," said Daniel. "Momentarily blinded by sunlight reflecting off a building, I miss a Stop sign and run over an old lady crossing the road. *That's* an accident." He sipped from the coffee mug. "In order to kill Elias the way I did, I *became* rage, filled myself with it. It was a choice, not an accident. When you abide in hatred, bad shit's gonna happen. Bottom line: I killed thirteen hundred people today. No, I didn't *intend* to, but intentions are bullshit—you know that." He looked straight at Pat. "I gotta say, Conrad's right about that much."

"So now what? You can't undo it."

"I can't deny I'm responsible for it, either. I just added a whole lot of innocent blood to my CV. I have to face that. But I have no idea what to do with it."

They sat in silence again.

"You'll get through it," said Pat.

"Yeah," said Daniel.

But would he? Calling it an accident, protesting his good intentions—that sort of rationalization was an insult to the dead. It compounded sin upon sin, and Daniel refused to indulge in it. Assuming he made it through this thing alive and sane, he would have to tell Kara what he'd done. Could she forgive him? Would she want him as a father to their child?

And how would he look into his child's eyes and offer a father's moral guidance, his own closet bursting with skeletons?

Pat gestured at the coffee mug on the table. "Wouldn't blame you if you wanted to crawl inside a bottle right now. I'd want to, and I don't even drink."

"I want to," said Daniel. "I can't. Maybe later." He lifted the ice bag off his wrist and dropped it on the table. "I keep thinking about why Conrad did what he did. Day my uncle died, Conrad visited me at Father Henri's place. He offered me a full Vatican pardon if I kept Tim from making that speech. Said if I allowed him to step onto the stage, I'd be in for a world of heartache. He wasn't bluffing. But now he just shows up to taunt me? Twist his mustache and gloat? Doesn't make sense. He didn't offer me anything, he didn't threaten me . . ."

"First, stop thinking of him as Conrad. Conrad was just a man."

"Pat, he's not a god."

"We don't know what he is," said Pat, "and it don't matter. He thinks he's a god, and he's got god-like power. So turn it around, look at it from the perspective of a dude named Noah with god-like power. Why would that guy show up to taunt you?"

Daniel thought about it. "Noah wanted to make me want exactly what I want right now. He told me I was too late—said it almost casually—but if I was really too late, there'd have been no reason for him to communicate with me at all. Why go to the trouble? He wants me to give up and climb into a bottle, because it's not too late and he knows I've got the pieces and I just haven't put them together."

"So put them together," said Pat.

Daniel looked into his coffee, breathed deep and slow, and quieted the internal chatter to focus on one thought at a time. "When I was on the pier with Elias, he said I was gonna die trying to protect a dream. And Noah said he was going to make a better dream. Not make *this* dream better." Daniel looked at Pat. "He doesn't want to improve the dream. He's gonna end it and start a new one."

"Well, shit," said Pat. He examined the label on his root beer for a few moments before looking up. "Guess we better stop him."

"Guess so."

"If you were Noah, how would you—"

"I'm thinking," said Daniel.

Pat nodded, waited.

Daniel said, "He's gonna make the ribbons touch—and the universe containing Earth will cease to be. How does he do that? He's exponentially more powerful than I am—and look what I did in a fit of pique. He could throw a temper tantrum in Source and lay utter waste to this planet . . . might make the dream a hellish nightmare, but obviously that's not enough to end it, or he'd have done it by now. So we can assume simple physical destruction, like a natural disaster, won't bring the ribbons together. Following me?"

"Just barely," said Pat.

Daniel said, "Look: think of this place as Earth—"

"That's easy enough, it *is* Earth."

"Okay—metaphor alert—think of this as Earth, and Source as the sun, which basically powers life on Earth, and you want to bring them together. Which do you move? Earth, right? So, to bring the ribbons together, *something* has to happen on this plane, or Noah would've done it from where he is. He's got a roomful of meditating monks in Source who at least believe they're influencing things here—and let's assume they are—and he's sending goons like Elias who can cross over and influence events on Earth. So, what kind of events could bring the ribbons closer? We know the ribbons are closest during periods of disruptive change in human affairs, and we know Elias, as Drapeau, operated in a world of the very highest geopolitical stakes, one that included plutocrats like the Council, moving dark money around to finance political instability."

Pat whistled. "It's like the Council's been lining up the dominos—they finance radical lunatics in oil-rich nations, hit South Carolina with a bioweapon, expanding the war across the Middle East, bankrupting Western democracy while they finance the rise of ultra-nationalists everywhere . . ."

Daniel said, "Dominos are stable, unless someone gives them a push. Conrad may not have known it at the time, but he set them up, and now Noah's gonna knock them down." The hair stood up on his forearms. "What would it take to trigger the next truly global war?"

He pushed his chair back and stood.

"We gotta get to New York."

31

Daniel walked through the park, past Bethesda Fountain and along the path toward the elegant cast-iron Bow Bridge. Trees bare and grass brown, but the day was sunny and unseasonably warm, so Daniel went gloveless and hadn't even bothered zipping his leather jacket.

Also made it easier to deploy his pistol, should the need arise.

He didn't really expect the need to arise.

No harm playing it safe.

He stepped onto the bridge. Ayo Onatade, head of the Foundation's AIT team, entered the bridge from the opposite shore. When they reached the middle, Daniel wrapped Ayo in a hug and kissed her cheek and Ayo hugged him back, but when they separated, she slapped his arm.

"Wayward boy," she said.

"For what it's worth"—Daniel smiled—"I've missed the hell out of you, Ayo."

"Of course you have. Who wouldn't?"

Daniel leaned against the railing and scanned the park. Office workers taking lunchtime power walks. A few tourists snapping pictures to post online for the folks back home. A couple in their fifties, arms intertwined, bodies touching, walking as one, strolling like time didn't exist. A group of excited schoolchildren on a Central Park field trip, harried teachers barely keeping them corralled.

Real people, living real lives.

"It's beautiful," said Daniel. "The park, even in winter."

"Especially in winter," said Ayo.

"Did you bring it?" said Daniel.

Ayo dug into her purse, pulled out a folded piece of paper, and handed it to Daniel. "That's him."

Daniel unfolded the photo and looked at the face of Jay Eckinsburger, the Foundation field operative who'd predicted Daniel's arrival in Source, and who'd gotten lost somewhere along the way.

It was the man Daniel had seen in the padded cell in Noah's tower.

Ayo said, "I'm afraid he'll be of no use to you. Hasn't uttered a word in ages."

"But he's conscious," said Daniel.

"Barely. He doesn't speak, doesn't react to anything at all. They put food in front of him and he'll eat a little, robotically, but that's it."

"Raoul said—"

"Raoul was just trying to get you to come back," said Ayo. "Jay never said what it was you might be able to stop, just that you could stop what he couldn't." She shivered. "It was the last thing he said."

Daniel handed the photo back. Eckinsburger had managed to be conscious in both places at once, but completely insane in both places at once.

Daniel's head swam. *Be there, or be here. Don't be both.*

Pat appeared behind Ayo and gave Daniel a nod, confirming the area was clear.

"Hey, darlin.'"

Ayo didn't miss a beat, turning her sights on Pat while accepting his embrace. "And as for you, Raoul is seriously displeased."

"He's always displeased."

"He said you're officially in his doghouse for running around after Drapeau while the world is falling apart, said to tell you he'll call when he returns from England and he expects you to answer the phone."

"Drapeau's dead," said Daniel. "He made a try for me and I killed him."

"Well, thank god for that," said Ayo. Then she turned all business. "I have very little time, boys. What's so important?"

"I lied to Raoul," said Daniel. "I've had AIT for some time, and I've seen . . . I can't get into how I know the things I know, and frankly you wouldn't believe me anyway. But in the next few days, something really bad is going to happen on Earth."

Ayo looked at him sideways. "On Earth."

"Somewhere, on Earth," said Daniel. "I mean, I don't know where on Earth it's gonna happen, or exactly when, or what it is. I realize that's vague—"

Ayo looked at Pat. "Is this boy joking?"

"Not even a little bit," said Daniel, "and whatever it is, it's imminent. I'm looking for plausible flash-point scenarios—nukes just gone missing, hard-nationalist uprisings, heightened terrorism chatter—something that could have massive military or geopolitical repercussions. Something that could trigger global war."

"Daniel, there's so much chatter these days we can barely keep up. And we've *always* got nukes missing—more than a hundred, at last count. Any one of them could go off in the next few days, and it could be anywhere—that's the definition of *missing*. So if the voices in your head aren't willing to be more specific than *something bad is going to happen somewhere on Earth*, I really can't help you." She looked at him with genuine sympathy. "I'm sorry, but I've got to get back to headquarters. We're stretched in a thousand directions right now."

Ayo turned to Pat. "If Wayward Boy's AIT says anything useful at all, I will hear from you without delay. Yes?"

"Yes, ma'am," said Pat.

"And when Raoul calls, play nice. We really need you back." Ayo reached out and touched the bruise on Daniel's neck. "Do take care of yourself. I worry about you."

She started to walk away. Daniel grabbed her arm.

"Wait. Raoul's not a field operative anymore. What's so important that's got him in England?"

She stiffened. "It shouldn't need stating that I'm not at liberty to share operational details with a former field op who, not so long ago, renounced his Foundation membership while holding our director at gunpoint. And it's unfair of you to ask."

She was right. Daniel searched for something—anything—that he'd learned in Source and that would make sense to her. He looked to Pat.

Pat shrugged.

Daniel said, "Ayo, I know the world is on the verge of something that can't be undone. I don't just have AIT like Tim and Kara and half a million more. I've got, like, AIT squared." To Pat: "Tell her. You've been with me the whole time."

Pat held Daniel's eye a moment, then turned to Ayo.

"It's true. Or, he's losing his mind. But I'm bettin' on the former."

"Thanks a heap," said Daniel. "Hell of an endorsement."

"What do you want me to say?" said Pat. "I said I'm betting on the former."

Ayo said nothing.

Daniel looked out at the sunlight shimmering on the water's surface. He said, "Conrad Winter—Conrad was just a bad dream compared to the guy I'm up against . . . the guy who sent Drapeau. And I promise you, he is about to unleash hell on humanity. So without revealing any operational details, tell me this: What would be the worst consequence, if a worst-case scenario unfolded at the thing Raoul's at in England?"

"What other geopolitical dominos would it knock over?" Pat added.

Ayo thought it through. Her face fell.

"Global war, isn't it?" said Daniel.

"It could be . . ." Ayo was silent for a moment, as she considered how much to share. "Raoul's at a trade summit, a private meeting—"

"Private, or secret?" said Pat.

She shot him a look. "Secret. The goal is to get agreement on the framework for a multilateral economic partnership prior to the G7. A handful of petroleum billionaires, a dozen European diplomats, several Eastern European heads of state. Some of the major players in the deal are Foundation allies, so we've got a security detail on-site. Raoul's running the team. But that summit is just one of hundreds of current potential flash points for global war."

"What we've been saying," said Pat. "The dominos are all set up, ready to tumble."

Daniel said, "Ayo, can you check if there's a Tudor chapel near the location of that summit?"

"I don't have to check—there's a chapel right inside the main building."

Daniel said, "Inside the chapel, there's a suit of armor, and a stained-glass portrait of Saint James the Apostle, writing in a blue Bible with a white feather quill."

Ayo stared at him, her mouth gaping.

"Oh my god," she said.

32

D amn it, damn it, damn it. No. All wrong."
Daniel held down the backspace key, *unsaying* everything,
again. For the sixth time.

Maybe the seventh would be the charm.

He started typing again.

> I was in San Diego. I was in your hotel, on the
> way to your room, when

When I filled my heart with rage and destroyed so many lives.

> —the earthquake hit. I tried to find you, but

But I had to run off and save the world.

> —I had to leave. I've been up to my ass in
> bad guys lately, and I'm still taking care of
> that, and

And if I fail, you and our unborn child and every living thing in the universe will cease to exist.

—we need to have the conversation we almost had in San Diego. I've attached a first-class ticket to London, where there's a room waiting for Dr. Maya Seth at Brown's Hotel. Come to London and settle in, and in a couple of days I'll join you, and we'll look into each other's eyes and tell truths.

I hope you'll use the ticket.

Love,
Me

He hit Send.

33

Kent, England

T he president of Latvia?" Daniel closed the briefing file Ayo had given him before they left New York.

Pat turned the wheel, leaving the A229, guiding the Range Rover onto a country road that ran into the woods ahead. "It's simple," he said. "The trade deal would basically turn a bunch of Baltic states into a mini-OPEC, giving them increased economic clout and more autonomy from Russia. Obviously, Russia—bankrupt without the income she now gets from the Baltic oil and gas trade—is against the deal. So you hit this summit, assassinate the president of Latvia, and leave some ginned-up evidence that points to Russia. Then you sit back with a Mai Tai and watch the rest of the dominos tumble."

"Right," said Daniel. "And Latvia's a member of NATO."

"It's like Archduke Ferdinand all over again," said Pat. "Nobody really gave a rat's ass about that dude, but the dominos were all lined up. British banks were in crisis, economy teetering on the brink of yet another depression, German economy on the rise, oil to be had from the weakening Ottoman Empire . . . treaties in place and wars to make money from. Old Franz was just the convenient first domino." He geared down as they approached the woods. "President of Latvia could serve the same function today. Anyway, that's who I'd pop if I were an assassin. But there's a half dozen others in attendance who might do the trick. Hell, Drapeau's replacement might be planning to take the whole place out with a dirty bomb, for that matter."

Just ahead, where the road turned to gravel and entered the woods, two six-foot stone pillars stood framing the road. The iron gate between them stood open. A brass plaque on the pillar to the left read:

ARLINGTON MANOR

About a car length beyond the pillars, four steel bollards, each about two feet in diameter, rose from the gravel road, blocking the way. Pat pulled to a stop and they rolled down the windows and looked into the camera lenses built into the pillars.

After a few seconds, the steel bollards slowly sank into the ground with a pneumatic hiss. Pat put the SUV in gear.

The gravel road ran through a thick woodland for about two miles, then opened onto an expanse of gently rolling meadow. In the center of the meadow stood an immaculately restored stone Tudor castle—dating from the 1530s, Daniel remembered from the briefing file. The road meandered ahead, winding through the meadow, limiting the speed of their approach.

✤ ✤ ✤

"Perfect." Daniel laughed as they drove across a small bridge. "It's actually moated."

"Be better with gators," said Pat.

The gravel road ended at the castle's front entrance, a stone fountain standing in the middle of the circular drive. Three other black SUVs lined the drive. A half dozen hard men patrolled the area, white cords curling from earpieces and snaking down behind collars, MP5s bulging under waxed Barbour coats.

Daniel and Pat stepped out of the car. Pat stretched his back, wincing slightly as a series of pops and cracks and crunches reverberated from his spine.

Pat said, "Forgot to tell you, old friend of yours joined the Foundation shortly after you left."

Daniel looked up at the approaching security man. Evan Sage.

Sage had been with the Department of Homeland Security, chasing down the same weaponized plague as Daniel. When their paths had crossed, Sage had not been gentle. Later, he'd tried to make up for it, securing Daniel an off-the-books flight to chase down Conrad Winter.

Sage held his hands up in mock surrender. "Don't break my nose, Daniel."

"Nah, we're even," said Daniel, shaking Evan's hand.

Sage said, "I heard what happened. You're a legend at the Foundation. I'm glad you got him."

Wouldn't be so glad if he knew Daniel hadn't just killed Conrad, but somehow elevated him to superhuman power, creating Noah.

"Well. Thanks for the plane," said Daniel.

Sage looked a little troubled. "I just want you to know, I am sorry about the waterboarding. That's not who I am, really. I just, I got a bit lost along the way."

"Found yourself at the Foundation, huh?"

Sage shrugged.

"Hope it works out for you," said Daniel.

Sage turned his head. "Uh-oh. Here he comes."

Raoul Aharon approached. He didn't look particularly happy.

"You are an asshole," Raoul said, pointing at Daniel.

"Nice to see you, Raoul," said Daniel.

"You should have told me from the beginning."

"This is not a conversation I'm willing to have," said Daniel.

"But now you suddenly remember who the good guys are?"

"Also not a conversation I'm willing to have."

"Raoul," said Pat, "Daniel's the reason we know there's gonna be an attempt tomorrow. Maybe you should start with *thank you*."

Whatever Raoul first wanted to say, he put it away with a sharp nod. He said, "For the record: well done with Drapeau." He gestured at Daniel's bruised but healing face. "Looks like you came out okay, Grasshopper."

I did. Didn't work out so well for the people of San Diego, though.

"I had a good sensei," said Daniel. And with that, the hatchet was buried, at least for the time being. Evan Sage remained outside at his post as Raoul led them into the castle.

They crossed the stone floor of the grand entrance, walked down the main hallway into a wood-paneled dining hall, complete with coats of arms, hanging tapestries, and four suits of armor, one standing sentry in each corner of the large room.

On one of the tables, Raoul unrolled an aerial photograph encompassing the entire meadow to the edge of the woods. The moated castle stood in the center of the photo. A compass arrow pointed to $\mathcal{N}$ at the top of the photo. It was from this direction that Daniel and Pat had arrived. A similar gravel road—but straight, not winding—led out from behind the castle, across the moat, and ran south through the meadow and into the woods on the other side.

Raoul waved his hand over the photo. "All this, and the woodland outside the photo, all the way to the road, is private property owned by our host, Lord Arlington. We control it all. The entire place has been swept for explosives, radioactivity, biological agents—the works." He dragged a finger through the air, following the gravel road to the front door. "There are only two ways in or out, aside from hiking through the woods, and we've got the woods covered by thermal scans.

"Our dignitaries arrive at 14:30 tomorrow. A convoy of hardened SUVs, coming in the same way you just did. Arrival is obviously our prime point of vulnerability. Lead car, middle car, and two follow-cars are all our security guys. Four dignitary cars ahead and behind the middle car. Each dignitary has three of his own security men." Raoul shook his head. "Fucking nightmare of political ego-stroking to get them all to agree we run security, but Lord Arlington made it happen. It was either that, or no summit. So it's on us. Once the assets are inside the castle walls, the vulnerability to a sniper ends. But like I said, the woods are covered, and we've got a drone eye in the sky, so I don't see how a sniper could get into a line-of-sight position."

"Attack from the air?" said Daniel.

Raoul shook his head. "We control ten square miles of airspace, got a battery of surface-to-air launchers on ready. Short of a full military assault, gentlemen, nobody gets in."

"What about the people already in?" said Pat.

"Minimal staff, everyone on the property vetted by the Foundation, and double vetted by MI5. And we handpicked the security team." He handed a list to Pat. "Hell, you recruited half these guys, and I think you've worked with most of them."

Pat scanned the list and nodded his approval.

Daniel stared at the photo, and for no reason he could identify, he remembered the feeling in the stairwell when Noah's predators were closing in for the kill.

To Raoul, he said, "Humor me a minute. What about, not a full military assault, but say, a dozen elite paramilitary? How would that go down?"

Raoul shrugged. "It would go down like twelve very dead elite paramilitary. They'd fail. Even if they made the kill, they'd never get off the property alive."

"Okay, they'd fail. But how would they stage the assault?"

Raoul pointed at the road winding to the front door. "The bridge in front is fixed, but in back it's a drawbridge, and it'll be up, so they'd have to make a frontal assault. The moat is electrified—we can run current through it—so you must cross the bridge to get in.

"But first, they'd have to get past our teams at the front gates. Remember those bollards when you came in? More bollards, every quarter mile, all the way to the moat, front and rear. And they'll split a car in half." He now pointed at the straight road leading from the back of the castle. "But if they got close enough to attack—which they wouldn't—we'd lower the drawbridge and evacuate our dignitaries out the back, where a dozen SUVs stand ready to roll at all times, and then the drawbridge and bollards would go up immediately behind them."

Pat clasped Raoul on the shoulder. "Even I gotta admit, looks like a solid setup."

A hard man almost as big as Pat bounded into the room wearing a sidearm and a big smile. "Chief! They didn't tell me you were joining the party!"

"Moondoggie!" said Pat. "How they hangin'?"

"You know how it is: The only easy day was yesterday." He clasped Pat's hand in his, gave him a hug with the other arm. "Got a minute to come say hi to the boys?"

"Good idea," said Raoul, but Pat and Moondoggie were already on their way out the door.

"I want to see the chapel," said Daniel.

"After Ayo told me about your vision, I had our guys sweep the chapel again," said Raoul. "Nothing. Place is clean."

"I want to see the chapel," Daniel repeated.

Raoul looked at him. "Oh. Yes, right. You think you might have one of those"—he wiggled his fingers beside his head—"AIT visions in there?"

"I don't know."

"Worth a try though, right?"

"Worth a try."

Raoul led them out of the dining hall and around a corner. "It's this way." As they walked, his expression changed, and he spoke quietly. "I told you for real, back at the hospital. I'm jealous of you,

Daniel. Not that I feel more worthy than you, but . . . what makes you so special? Why were you chosen by AIT, and not me?" He snorted a laugh. "But then I remember your uncle had it, and I know it has nothing to do with *worthy*. No offense."

"None taken," said Daniel.

They came to a stop outside the chapel door.

Raoul said, "I don't think you appreciate how lucky you are to have it."

Daniel said, "Yeah, I'm lucky. I found a beautiful world run by a malevolent demigod who plans to destroy our universe, I got my one friend there killed, and when I tried to fight back I murdered thirteen hundred people in San Diego. I'm havin' a fuckin' blast."

But not out loud.

Out loud, he said, "It's not as much fun as you think."

⁂

The chapel was exactly as it had appeared in the hologram above the meditators. Dark beams and carved pews, a large wooden cross, a suit of armor next to the stained-glass portrait of Saint James the Apostle.

Daniel stood alone at the altar and looked across the empty pews.

He wanted to ask for help.

He wanted to pray.

But he couldn't.

His eye was drawn back to the portrait of Saint James, holding a Bible the same color as Tim Trinity's.

Faith without works is dead.

Daniel remembered himself as a nine-year-old boy, the year he had a dog, lying in bed, praying to God. Praying for what he always prayed for, when his prayers were earnest. Praying for God to reveal himself. Daniel so needed to believe his uncle was not a con man but a servant of the Lord. He'd been raised on the lie and believed it when he was younger, and the world had been a strange and magical place then, but as he grew his mind rebelled against believing what he knew wasn't so. And on that night, Daniel prayed with hot tears burning his face, because on that night, Daniel was offering God a deal.

A sacrifice.

"Just show yourself, just once, and I'll never ask again. And I'll pay. If I wake up in the morning and Judas is—" He choked back a sob as he stroked the scruffy mutt lying next to him in bed. "You can take my dog. And then I'll know you're real. I'll pay the price."

He awoke the next morning with Judas licking his face, and he hugged the mutt and cried, overwhelmed by relief. And shame.

Daniel had spent most of his life searching for proof, constitutionally unable as he was to abide in faith. Funny, a priest without faith, but that's what he'd become, casting the world aside, denying himself a normal life, on a single-minded mission to find a miracle, to see God's face.

Just once, and then he'd be free.

But there had been no miracles.

At least, not until his search brought him back around to his estranged uncle, and Daniel saw AIT for the first time, entering a world of questions without answers, leaving the priesthood behind, determined to follow the questions where they led, no longer searching for the face of God, but for the truth, whether that truth included a god or not.

He discovered a beautiful world called Source where reality runs on attention and intention, and where you can't ignore the feelings of others. A strange and magical place where he'd spend half his life if he could bring Kara and their child, or visit if he couldn't. He could spend weeks in Source and only be gone an hour. All the time in the world.

A beautiful world, but for Noah.

You gonna save us? Huck had asked Daniel.

I'm gonna try.

Daniel wanted to ask for help.

He wanted to pray.

But he couldn't.

In the end, Daniel's lifetime search had led him to Source, to uncertainty as the *only* certainty regardless of existential discomfort, and to the notion that there wasn't much difference between yearning to see God and yearning to be God.

Praying just didn't make sense to him anymore.

Still, he wanted to ask for help.

He looked back to the stained-glass Saint James, writing in Tim Trinity's blue Bible. The portrait appeared to shimmer for a moment and Daniel thought he could taste cinnamon, but it passed so quickly he decided he'd imagined it.

He wondered if Noah's followers were meditating on the chapel right now.

Wondered if Noah could see him.

He stepped down from the altar and stood in the middle of the room, facing the stained glass.

"I didn't quit, Noah," he said aloud. "I didn't quit, and I figured you out. And you're not a god. You're just a sad man who wants to be God. And I am awash in sin, but I'm not gonna let you win tomorrow."

He walked between the pews all the way to the door, turned back to face the chapel. He said, "And there's absolutely nothing you can do to stop me, because you can't cross over. And this is not a dream."

34

Most of the guests at the Arlington Inn had no idea they were staying fewer than ten miles from the most secure property in Kent. Catering primarily to bird watchers, the old hotel in town played the role of hospitable country squire perfectly. A tweedy old man stood behind the hand-carved reception desk, oversized room keys hanging on wall hooks behind him. A couple of resident English Spaniels flaked out on green tartan dog beds, and a fire crackled in the lobby's stone fireplace. Just off the lobby, a cozy library bar, shelves crammed with popular fiction, local histories, and books on ornithology.

Daniel unpacked in his room, then ate dinner alone in the library bar. Pat had stayed to go over details with the security team, and Raoul had ordered Daniel to bed early, adding a dig about how exhausted he looked.

Getting on local time was a good idea, in theory, but Daniel had lived in perpetual jet lag since flying to Barcelona . . . when was that, a week ago?

He couldn't remember. Anyway, it was nothing compared to the jet lag between Earth and Source.

Still, he had to do what he could. So he ate a dinner he could barely taste because he needed the nutrition. And he limited himself to one glass of red wine, and a wee dram of Laphroaig for dessert. The same single malt he'd shared with Kara on the south coast of Norway, the night of their first kiss.

A beautiful night.

Source was beautiful, but Earth was also beautiful, despite Pat's commitment to cynicism. Pat wasn't wrong about the ugliness and cruelty in the world. But there was also beauty, so much it sometimes made Daniel's chest ache.

And there was Kara. And a child on the way.

Daniel tipped back his glass, filling his mouth with whisky. Not as strong as he'd remembered, certainly a shadow of what it would be in Source, but he could taste the smokiness of it and it was pretty damn good.

Worth fighting for.

He checked his watch: almost eight o'clock. He signed the bill and headed into the lobby. Before he got to the stairs, Pat entered from outside.

"You eaten?" said Pat.

Daniel nodded. "Just heading to bed. Big day tomorrow."

"Good. You can sleep 'til nine, that'll get you almost twelve hours."

"Do I look that tired?"

"Yeah, man, you do. Raoul's letting you on-site tomorrow in case you have a vision that helps, but he's not thrilled about it. Said to tell you if you show up before noon, he'll have you shot."

"Fine," said Daniel.

"Listen, I'm gonna grab dinner with the boys, engage in a little pre-battle bonding."

"Have fun." Daniel said. "Tell the boys *Oorah* for me."

"*Hooyah*," said Pat. "*Oorah* is for pussies." He started for the door. "See ya in the a.m."

Daniel climbed the stairs to his room, feeling a smile invade his face.

Noon tomorrow.

He opened his laptop on the bed, got online, and checked his email, pulse pounding in his wrist against the edge of the keyboard.

The email from Kara contained only two words, but they were exactly the words Daniel needed to read.

In London.

He hit Reply.

✦ ✦ ✦

He dreamed of Source. Dreamed of the warm late-afternoon sun and the sound of the gentle surf. Dreamed of spot-traveling through the seaside town, down to the beach where Digger had once introduced him to the creative potential of the uncertainty principle.

A boy stood on the beach.

Huck.

The boy said, "I tried to call you back here."

"It worked," said Daniel.

"I had a vision. I met Tim Trinity. He said he was your uncle. Is that true?"

Daniel felt lightheaded.

"Yes, it is."

"He told me to manifest this and give it to you." Huck dug in his pocket and held out a blue rabbit's foot, a single key on the brass keychain.

Daniel took it from Huck's hand. He read his own initials where he'd scratched them on the brass after attaching his house key to the chain. Tim Trinity had bought it for him in a souvenir shop at Stone Mountain when they visited for Daniel's seventh birthday. When Daniel still believed his uncle was God's chosen messenger, and the world was still a strange and magical place.

"I don't know what it means," said Huck, "but I figured I should give it to you."

Daniel put the rabbit's foot in his pocket, and—

The dream ended. He opened his eyes.

The bedside clock read three a.m.

He rolled onto his other side, closed his eyes again, and fell back into a fitful sleep, the taste of cinnamon fading on his tongue.

35

*T*oday *is a good day to die. But I've decided to stay alive until tomorrow.*

Daniel opened his eyes and sat for a few seconds, then rose from zazen and drew the curtains wide. Unrelenting cloud cover pressed down on the Earth like a heavy pewter blanket, promising rain.

He'd been careful with his morning meditation and stayed with breath counting, not wanting to risk going too deep in case he accidentally crossed over into Source.

Or woke up.

Earth was continuing to feel unreal, increasingly so, and Daniel had awakened remembering the dream with Huck, and he couldn't decide if it had really been a dream or if he'd been to Source in his sleep. But how could Huck have had a vision of Tim? And did the decreasing sense of reality here mean that Earth was a dream, or that Daniel was leaving more of his consciousness in Source with each visit? Or did it mean the worlds were growing closer, ribbons almost touching?

He had to stop the cacophony of these questions and the many others they raised. He knew he was at risk of spiraling—*getting lost,* as Digger had called it in Source.

Sometimes people on Earth got lost, too, and just before Daniel closed his eyes and stilled his mind, he thought of Jay Eckinsburger, who got lost in both places.

The meditation was a risk he had to take, and the breath counting had worked well enough, and he now went through his kata routine with a relatively quiet mind.

Then a hot shower, blasting cold for the final minute.

He took stock in the mirror while shaving. Mirror-Daniel had a scab where his lip had split, a lively bruise on his left cheekbone, and another on the side of his neck. Also, heavy black bags under both eyes and at least a dozen new gray hairs.

"This can't be how thirty-four is supposed to look," Daniel said to Mirror-Daniel. He shaved extra close in a futile attempt to compensate.

And he put on cologne.

Pat rapped on the door as Daniel was tying his tie. Daniel flipped the latch and Pat came in carrying a small black Pelican case.

"Jacket 'n tie?" He looked at Daniel askance. "You know today might possibly involve some runnin' and gunnin', right?"

"I'll change after breakfast."

"Shucks, you don't gotta get all gussied up on my account."

"I'm having breakfast with Kara," said Daniel. "You're on your own, I'm afraid." He leaned into Pat's personal space, then backed out. "You think I went too heavy with the cologne?"

Pat stared at him for more than a few seconds before speaking. "You're not pullin' my leg, are you? She actually came to London."

"That she did."

Pat made no effort to hide his dismay. "Have you lost your freakin' mind? You have got to be on-site at noon. London's more than sixty miles from here, and what if you get stuck in traffic?"

"Dude, relax. She rented a car. I'm meeting her at the little faux-French café across the street. We'll have a couple croissants and a press pot of coffee, maybe Edith Piaf will be playing in the background. I'll pour my heart out—maybe it'll get broken, maybe not—and I'll be back before eleven and still have an hour to twiddle my thumbs before I'm allowed on-site."

Pat spoke as if addressing a child. "Let me explain. You can't effectively run 'n gun around the castle while moping over a broken heart. Just leave it 'til after, and get your head in the game."

"I might die today—I can accept that. But I can't be thinking, *I passed up the chance to tell her how I feel and now she'll never know* while I'm out there. So what I'm doing is getting my head in the game."

Pat thought about it, grudgingly conceded. "Fair enough, I guess you're right. I'll be downstairs in the car at eleven thirty. You can dry your tears on the drive over."

"I'll be ready," said Daniel.

Pat put the case on the desk. "But first, we shoot up. Lose the jacket a second." He pushed his own sleeve up, opened the case, and pulled out two pre-loaded syringes. "High-test antibiotic cocktail, special delivery from Foundation HQ."

Daniel remembered Kara injecting them both in the Foundation jet, on the way to South Carolina just before Conrad Winter's team crop-dusted the general population with a weaponized plague, plunging the state—and then the nation—into chaos, and pinning the attack on Yemeni terrorists.

Injecting himself, Pat said, "Nobody'd believe Russia would launch a biological attack on British soil to stop a trade deal, but we don't *know* Russia's the intended patsy. You could link it to Gulf state terrorism or religious lunatics, I suppose. Not what I would do, but . . ." He pulled the needle out of his arm, returned it to the case.

Daniel said, "Either way, we know it's in Conrad's bag of tricks, which means it's in Noah's bag of tricks." He removed his jacket and laid it on the bed, rolled up his sleeve, started pumping his left fist. "I'll do me."

Daniel held out his hand and Pat gave him the other syringe, and he flipped the orange cap off the needle. He didn't see any bubbles, but he held the syringe pointy end up and flicked it with his fingernail a few times, just to be safe. He picked a good vein, injected himself, and handed the syringe back, and Pat returned it to the case and snapped the case shut.

Daniel rolled his sleeve down and slipped back into his jacket. He straightened his tie and spread his hands to his sides.

"How do I look? And feel free to lie."

Pat said, "You look like hell, but you smell lovely. Just the right amount of cologne."

"Wish me luck."

Daniel took two steps toward the door but then his legs stopped cooperating. He tried to force the next step, but his leg wouldn't move. He felt himself wobble in place.

Pat reached a hand out to steady him.

"Easy there. Maybe you should sit down."

Daniel's body didn't give him a choice. He sat hard on the floor, leaning back against the bed. He couldn't taste cinnamon and he wasn't spontaneously crossing over—this felt different—but for a moment he could only think of the fact that he was going to stand Kara up.

Again.

Then he turned his head and looked at the case holding the empty syringes.

Pat said, "You gotta let me explain."

Daniel's body was becoming a distant thing. He couldn't lift his arms. When he tried, his hands slipped off his thighs and came to rest on the rug.

"Pat?"

Pat sat on the floor across from Daniel and lit a cigarette. He said, "It's a temporary paralytic of sorts. Your body'll go numb for about ten minutes, then you'll pass out for a brief spell. I promise, after a nap you'll wake feeling bright-eyed and bushy-tailed. Believe me, it's in your best interest to sit this one out."

Daniel didn't feel the urge to sleep, not yet, but he realized his brain function was somewhat compromised and he had to force himself to stop focusing on the fact that he now couldn't feel the rug under his palms.

They sat and looked at each other without speaking, and it occurred to Daniel that Pat was waiting for him to put it together.

Oh. Shit.

"What are you gonna do, Pat?"

"Come on, man, you know what I'm gonna do."

"What are you going to do?"

"I'm gonna shoot the president of Latvia in the fuckin' head and start the next global war. Where ya been?"

"But . . . why?"

"Because Noah's right." Blue smoke rose like ghost worms from the cigarette between Pat's fingers. "Because we're hardwired to remain savages, and there's no making this a better dream. Human beings are just no damn good. Time to end this dream and start a new one."

Daniel said, "This can't be happening," but he knew that it was. He tried to think of what to say, how to reach Pat. He bought time with, "Listen to me: and remember, this is your best friend talking—"

But Pat wasn't listening. "It's all right. Just the end of a bad dream." He snapped his fingers. "Opportunity for a better one."

"When did Noah get to you?"

"Does it matter?"

"Yes. It does."

Pat shook his head. "I don't have AIT and I can't cross over, but Noah's got more followers in the dream than you realize. His emissaries have recruited thousands more than just those who sometimes wake up in Source. They reached me a few months back, explained Source and the dream, and it all just made sense."

"This is not a dream! Kara is real. My unborn child is real."

"Sure, I'm real, too. But deep inside, I've always known I'm dreaming and I just can't wake up. Never will. Like most people."

"Doesn't matter if it's just a dream," said Daniel. "It's the only dream we've got."

"And take a good look at it!" Pat spat the words out like spoiled food. His eyes flashed fire. "It's not a dream, it's a fuckin' snuff film.

A charnel house." He flicked his cigarette, sending ash to the floor. "Spent my whole life fighting secret wars, killing other human beings, tellin' myself I was spreading the blessings of democracy. Complete and utter bullshit. I was killing so we can continue suckin' wealth from the same people we conquered hundreds of years ago and kept down ever since. We disguise it, but our luxury, to this very day, is provided by the slaver's whip."

Pat's eyes grew moist and he took another deep drag on the cigarette, regaining control. "We had the whole goddamn world, and look what we made with it. And you can spare me the *but look how far we've come*, and the *what about love and laughter and art and music and science and children and puppies and rainbows*—that's just you trying to let humanity off the hook. Face it: We suck. Tell me I'm wrong."

Daniel said, "Pat, I love you and I'm telling you straight. Your head is broken—something's gone wrong with your mind."

"You're one to talk."

Daniel could feel sleep waving at him from a distance. How much longer did he have, and what could he say, or was Pat too far gone to reach?

He said, "All those oppressed people we treat so badly—did you ask their opinion before deciding to end their entire existence? Do they get a vote?"

Pat said, "You still don't get it. And you don't even see how important you are, man. You're stuck trying to defend a bad dream, and you're missing what comes next. The present is the future of the past—it has to be—but it doesn't have to be the past of the future. We end this dream so the next dream can be born unburdened by history."

"Is that what Noah's emissaries told you? And you think he's gonna dream puppies and rainbows, unburdened by history? You think a guy like Conrad Winter is gonna create a dream of Paradise?"

"No." Pat crushed his cigarette out on the floor. "But you can, my brother." His eyes sparkled like he was reliving a moment of spiritual epiphany. "Soon as you told me about meeting Dana Cameron in a vision, I knew you'd been to Source, and it hit me. You're the one, you're the one who can do it. You can balance Noah's power. You're more powerful than you realize."

Sleep, no longer content to wave from a distance, began its approach. Daniel's eyes grew heavy. He fought against it. Pat stood and stretched his back, a series of pops and cracks sounding up and down his spine. Then a grinding, bone-on-bone crunch as he moved his right arm in a circle. A body that had fought too many battles. A man who had seen too much horror and done too much harm.

"My dream is over, Daniel, but yours is just beginning. Go back to Source. Grow strong, and help shape the next dream." Pat stepped close and leaned over and kissed Daniel on the top of the head. "Make it a good one."

Daniel's eyes fell shut.

36

Sound returned first.

Heavy rain, sheeting down, lashing against the windowpane. Then, a man's calm voice. English accent. The radio on the desk, playing at full volume.

Middlesbrough, two; Manchester United, nil.

Thunder boomed outside.

Crystal Palace, one; Bournemouth, five.

Thunder again—three short bursts in quick succession.

Tottenham Hotspur, four; Chelsea, nil.

Three more bursts, but it wasn't thunder, it was someone rapping hard on the door, and Daniel finally surfaced and opened his eyes and tried to sit up, and learned painfully that his wrists and ankles were bound to the bedframe with plastic zip ties.

Hull City, two; Arsenal, one.

And his mouth was gagged. With his own tie.

Three more hard raps on the door.

Daniel turned his head. The bedside clock read 1:41 p.m. He did the math. Forty-nine minutes until the dignitaries arrived. Driving time, hotel to the front gate of Arlington Manor: nine minutes, at a good clip.

There was still time.

Another rap, and then Kara spoke through the door.

"I sat on a plane for eleven hours."

Daniel called out her name, but the gag muffled his voice and the radio was loud and the old hotel had thick walls.

"Damn it, Daniel." Silence. "Okay. I give up. I can't do this anymore."

"Kara!"

But she couldn't hear him.

And Daniel couldn't hear Kara's footsteps, but he knew she was walking away.

"Kara!"

Nothing.

Only the rain.

And *Liverpool, three; Everton, one.*

Daniel screamed and jerked against the zip ties, welcoming the pain, pushing into it until his wrists were slick with blood and he collapsed back on the bed.

Defeated and utterly alone.

It was all over. Kara was gone, and Pat was beyond repair. And Daniel could do nothing. Nothing to stop Pat from triggering a global war. Nothing to keep the ribbons apart. Nothing to save this world—this dream, however good, however bad, the only dream we've got.

And nothing to stop Kara from walking away.

He pictured her stomping down the stairs and crossing the lobby, leaving the hotel and walking fast to her rental car—not crying, not yet, not until she was inside the car, damn it. And she couldn't believe Daniel would do this, it was such a betrayal after she'd come—

Wait.

He could *feel* what Kara was feeling. He didn't think he was imagining it. And she'd had AIT. Maybe . . .

You're more powerful than you realize.

Daniel squeezed his eyes tight. He reconnected to Kara's emotional pain, locked on to it. Then he projected a mental image of himself bound to the bed.

See me. Come on, Kara. See me . . .

Something changed. Yes, betrayed, angry, but . . . confused.

He bore down on it.

Help me . . .

He felt her confusion grow urgent, and he didn't know if he was really connecting or if it was just wishful thinking, but he pictured her running back into the hotel and grabbing a key from the wall hooks behind the reception desk and running up the stairs and—

Kara flung the door wide.

"Oh my god!" She ran to his side.

"Mmumph!" he said.

Watford, nil; Southampton, nil, said the man on the radio.

Kara loosened the knot and worked the silk tie out of Daniel's mouth. "I can't believe it—I saw this! I saw you lying here and I felt, like, this desperate need and I almost didn't come back because I thought, *This is crazy*, but then it kept getting stronger and I knew I couldn't just leave and not know and—"

"Kiss me," said Daniel.

She did. "Who did this to you?"

"Pat."

"What? Why would—"

"Long story, tell ya later," said Daniel. He jerked his head in the direction of the bathroom. "Toenail clippers, dopp kit, bathroom. Please."

"Right." She disappeared into the bathroom.

And now we turn to Championship League. Wolverhampton, three; Wigan Athletic, one.

Kara reemerged with Daniel's toenail clippers in hand.

"Could you please shut that guy up?" said Daniel.

He watched as she crossed to the radio and switched it off. Her pregnancy was showing—not obvious at first glance, but there was a slight roundness under the untucked silk blouse, and something about the way she stood.

She caught him admiring her body and hovered over him with the clippers in her hand and a devilish look on her face.

"If I cut you loose, are you gonna disappear on me again?"

He said, "Cut me loose and find out."

She clipped his wrists free first, then his ankles, and as he sat up she sat next to him on the bed. "If your next words are 'I gotta go . . .'"

He kissed her long and hard and he held her tight. Then saw the mess he was making with his bloody wrists, and he pulled back.

"I just wrecked your shirt."

"I don't care."

Daniel stood up, and she rose with him. He put a hand lightly on her pregnant belly.

He said, "I want this child. And I want you. And I know you think we haven't been together long enough, so if you want to live together first, I'll do that. Or I'll live across the street and we can go steady. Whatever it takes. I think Maya Seth and Ian Shefras can be happy together, and you think it's possible, too, or you wouldn't be standing in front of me right now and you sure as hell wouldn't be wearing that makeup. There's so much between us, lady, it'd be a crime not to at least give it a chance. I recorded a long voice-mail but I didn't send it because you're right about doing this face-to-face. But you'd have liked it, I think. It was a good voice-mail. I even paraphrased that poem by e.e. cummings."

Kara's eyes welled up and her full lips broke into a wide smile.

Daniel said, "But right now, I actually do have to go."

She laughed. "Must be important. Gotta run off and save the world?"

"Actually, yes."

Kara's smile vanished. She knew he wasn't kidding. She'd been caught in the war for AIT, she'd stood over the pit of bodies in Liberia, and she'd treated thousands of victims of the biological attack on South Carolina. She'd almost been collateral damage herself.

She said, "Why are you still standing here?" Then kissed him and pointed at the hallway. "Go."

"Girl of my dreams," said Daniel. "Can I borrow your car?"

37

The dashboard clock read 2:09 p.m.

Twenty-one minutes.

Daniel slowed as he approached the stone pillars. He squinted through the fogged windshield, past hyperactive wiper blades and into the sheeting rain. The iron gates were closed. Two Range Rovers beside the gates, four men in each car. One team would stay at the gate, the other would fall in behind the dignitaries and become the second follow-car to the convoy from here to the castle.

There's still time.

Daniel pulled to a stop and put the car in park but left the engine running. He rolled down his window and drew a deep breath. One of the security men stepped out and trudged through the rain to Kara's car, nodding as he recognized Daniel. Two men got out of the other Range Rover, one leading a German shepherd, the other unfolding an angled mirror at the end of a metal pole. They began walking around the car, Mirror checking the undercarriage, Dog sniffing for explosives.

"Afternoon, Mr. Byrne."

"Where's Pat?" Daniel tried to sound calm.

"Checked in a while ago, I think he's with Raoul in the dining hall." The man reached for his radio. "I can raise him on coms—"

"That's okay," Daniel said, as casually as he could, "I'll just catch up with him." He gestured toward the gate.

"Yes, sir. Please lower all your windows, pop the trunk and the hood . . ."

"I'm alone," said Daniel as he lowered the windows.

"I'm sure you are. We still gotta look."

"Of course." Daniel reached down and pulled the trunk release and popped the hood.

The German shepherd jumped in through the rear passenger-side window, sniffed Daniel, sniffed around the cabin, jumped back out, leaving the smell of wet dog behind.

One of the men checked under the hood. The other looked in the trunk. Daniel drummed his fingers on the steering wheel, blew out a breath. These men were trained to recognize signs of nervousness, and Daniel reminded himself to stay cool. But every second seemed an hour, and how long could it take to search a car's trunk? He took another deep breath and blew it out slowly.

After what felt like a year, hood and trunk both thunked shut. The first man spoke a few words into his radio, and the gates swung open.

Daniel drove through the woods faster than he should have and not fast enough, playing it through in his mind. "Raoul, I know you and Pat have fought together for years and trust each other with your lives, and I know you definitely don't trust me after I broke into Ames's house and held him at gunpoint, but listen: Pat's gone rogue. He's working with Conrad Winter, and I know Conrad's dead, but now he's a malevolent demigod named Noah living in the Source universe, and Pat's gonna shoot the president of Latvia in the head and start World War Three, and that'll provide the final push needed to bring the ribbons together—"

Maybe not.

Pat's drug had worn off and Daniel's mind was clear enough to know there was no way in hell to make Raoul believe Pat had gone rogue, never mind explaining Conrad/Noah and Source and ribbons.

Daniel drove out of the woods and into the meadow, slowed by the now-winding road.

He made a to-do list.

One: Figure out how and where, exactly, Pat is planning to shoot the president of Latvia.

Two: Get there and confirm.

Three: Call in the cavalry and stop Pat.

He glanced at the clock. Twelve minutes to complete three simple tasks.

Daniel's mind was clear, but as he continued along the gravel road, the sense of unreality he'd fought off earlier—the feeling that this was all a dream—threatened to rise anew. The scenery didn't help. A moated castle rising from the meadow, all colors muted under the blanketing sky, visibility shortened by the rain, distant features fading to gray mist.

Be here now. Surf the wave.

He drove across the fixed bridge over the moat, pulled to a stop in the circular drive, and took a few long, centering breaths. Several members of the security team patrolled the vicinity on foot. Daniel stepped out of the car and was instantly soaked. He jogged through the cold rain to the man at the front door.

"Where's Pat?" said Daniel.

"Conducting a perimeter check."

"Raoul?"

"Dining hall."

Daniel jogged to the dining hall, where he found Raoul and Evan Sage watching video feeds from around the property on a stack of monitors.

Raoul looked up, leaving monitor duty to Sage, as Daniel approached. "Pat said you weren't feeling well."

"Where is he?" said Daniel.

"Perimeter. Just radioed, on his way back." Raoul glanced at his watch. "Cutting it a little close, they'll be here in eight minutes." He scooped a radio from the table and stepped forward. "Channel One reaches everyone, Two is just the gate teams, Three is castle team, Four is convoy." He handed the radio to Daniel. "Channel Five is just you and me, Grasshopper. If AIT hits you and you see anything at all about this attack, you call it straight to me and we assess it, before we send everyone scrambling."

Daniel nodded. "I'm expecting a gunshot from a distance, but it's just a feeling at this point."

"We're covered for snipers. But you learn anything more specific—"

"I'll call you on Five."

Daniel clipped the radio to his belt.

✠ ✠ ✠

He stood in the chapel, facing Saint James the Apostle and Tim Trinity's royal-blue Bible.

Faith without works is dead.

Daniel tried to focus on Task One. What was Pat planning? All of the security SUVs were equipped with long guns, and going on a perimeter check allowed Pat to get away from the others, so a gunshot from a distance wasn't much of a leap. But from where? The rear walls of the castle cut off sightlines from the south, and the front meadow was wide open, nowhere to hide, and the woods were covered by thermal scans.

Jesus, Pat. What happened to you?

Daniel felt a sharp stab of grief for his broken best friend, for the man Pat had been before it all went so wrong. And guilt for having missed it. Why hadn't he seen it coming?

Pat's world view had darkened dramatically in the last year, but so had Daniel's, after all they'd seen. And so had everyone's, for that matter. The world hadn't exactly enjoyed a banner year—or a banner decade, as Pat so regularly mentioned.

Like many men, Pat was prone to dressing his fears in humor, and Daniel had thought the hyper-cynical rants were just a coping mechanism.

But they were much more than that. Pat had been selling Daniel, one rant at a time, on the idea that the dream of Earth was fatally flawed, irredeemable, unworthy of saving. He'd been *grooming* Daniel for his role in the whole twisted plan, while keeping him close until the point of no return.

Daniel snapped to and checked his watch. Five minutes. He depressed his radio's Talk button.

"Raoul, is Pat back yet? Over."

"No. Over."

"Well, where is he? Over."

"Daniel, I'm busy. Pat slid off the road in the mud and hit a tree. Truck won't start, he's walking in. Over."

"Did you see it happen? Is he on the monitors? Over."

"We had him on thermal until he cleared the south woods. He's off camera now. Pat's a big boy, he can look after himself. Now I don't want you in my ear again unless you're channeling the Amazing Kreskin, you got that? Over and out."

South woods. No clear shot from that direction.

Whatever Pat was doing, he was doing it off camera and there was no way to find him until he reemerged.

Daniel felt utterly powerless.

Wait. Pat's only half the equation—the other half is provided by Noah and his army of meditators in Source.

Could Daniel stop it from Source?

If I can get to the meditators, maybe I can disrupt the meditation—

But even if Daniel were successful, even if he crossed over directly into the meditation hall and could somehow break the meditation, then he'd be in Source and there'd be no one here to stop Pat from triggering global war.

It was an impossible situation.

Unless . . .

Unless I can be in both places at the same time.

Daniel's stomach roiled at the very idea, and he had to fight not to vomit.

He caught a mental flash of Jay Eckinsburger standing in frozen terror in Source, drooling on himself in a near-catatonic state on Earth. Jay, who'd managed to be in both places at once.

It had cost the man his sanity, but it clearly wasn't impossible.

Bifurcating his consciousness to put himself in both places might mean Daniel would have to spend the rest of his life in a straitjacket in both places—but that now seemed a small price to pay.

Faith without works is dead.

Daniel focused his attention on the stained-glass window in front of him. Saint James the Apostle, holding Tim Trinity's blue Bible.

He remembered the meditation hall in Noah's tower, made a mental picture of it, thinking: *If you can see a place, you can be there.*

Daniel strained to hold two competing realities in his mind at the same time. Tried to *feel* himself standing in the chapel, while also feeling himself standing in the meditation hall in Source. Tried to make both ideas equally real.

And as he did so, the stained glass in front of him grew brighter and began emitting a bright white shimmering light.

Glimmer.

Daniel's mouth flooded with the taste of cinnamon as the glimmer flashed so bright he had to close his eyes.

When he opened them, Saint James the Apostle and Tim's Bible were not there. Instead of looking at a stained-glass window, he was looking through a shimmering haze, a window directly into Source.

The meditation hall in Noah's tower.

It looked like Noah's entire flock—two thousand people filling the hall, sitting with their eyes closed, palms upturned, sitting on little red chairs, packed into tight rows.

There was a man standing beside the flock.

The man walked forward.

Daniel walked forward.

As the man got closer, he began to look familiar.

Daniel stopped walking and stood just a foot from the membrane.

The remaining haze cleared. The man on the other side stared at Daniel.

Daniel raised his hand to his mouth. It was exactly what he wanted, exactly what he'd intended, but for a moment he was unable to make sense of what he was seeing.

He was seeing—

—himself, in Source, raising his hand to his mouth, unable to make sense of what he was seeing.

38

Daniel lowered his hand from his mouth. He stared up at the hologram hanging above Noah's followers. At himself.

The version of himself in the Tudor chapel stared back, also lowered his hand from his mouth, looking every bit as shocked. Then Hologram-Daniel whipped his head to the side, attention drawn away. He turned and sprinted out of the chapel.

Raoul had said Pat was near the south woods. That had meant something, but what? And—

Stop. Recalibrate. You're in Source now—at least this part of you is. You can't chase Pat, that's the other Daniel's job.

Daniel felt lightheaded. Yes, this is what he'd intended, but still his mind reeled, questions flooding in faster than he could focus.

How can I be in both places? Because Digger was right; I've always been in both places. But will I be able to get back? Can I ever be the other Daniel again? Am I stuck here now? And what will—?

He closed his eyes, took a deep breath.

Be here now.

He opened his eyes again and took stock. With Noah's entire flock in attendance, the hologram was much larger—huge, compared with the last time he was here. He looked at the sea of people sitting in silence just a few feet away, all in deep meditation, oblivious to his presence. No, something beyond that. This was more than meditation; these people were almost . . . somewhere else. Daniel could probably split their skulls with a meat cleaver and they wouldn't even notice.

He took a step toward them, and the dome of light that powered the hologram stretched lower as he did, an energy barrier preventing any further approach, making it impossible to disrupt their meditation. The light wasn't glimmer exactly, and Daniel could look at it. He could almost see structure in it, but constantly shifting and reshaping, kaleidoscopic in nature. This was the energy sent by Noah to power the meditation, but the way it moved to keep Daniel out seemed automatic, not consciously directed.

Go back to Source, Pat had said. *Grow strong, and help shape the next dream.*

But Daniel wasn't here to set in motion the next dream. He was here to save the flawed and fragile dream we've already got, and there was no time to grow strong. Whatever strength he had now would either be enough—or it wouldn't.

He took one last look at the hologram. The chapel on Earth, where the other version of himself had stood before sprinting off to stop his broken best friend from knocking over the first domino of Armageddon.

"Good luck, Daniel," he said. "We're both gonna need it."

He turned from the hologram and entered the stairwell, spot-traveled up to the next landing, and did it again.

Now he stood at the door to the heart of Noah's world, and he could feel Noah's confidence clearly through the door. But for some reason Noah still hadn't noticed him, even at this distance.

He reached for the door handle. Locked. He thought back. When Noah had appeared before Daniel in San Diego, he'd surrounded himself with plain white walls. Daniel had no idea what was on the other side of this door. Without the ability to picture it in his mind, there was no way to spot-travel there.

How could he have come this far, even bifurcating his consciousness between two worlds, only to be stopped by a locked door?

He stared at the keyhole.

Then he remembered.

Daniel reached into his pocket and pulled out the blue rabbit's-foot keychain Huck had given him on the beach.

He slid the key into the lock.

Thanks, Tim.

39

D aniel stood in the chapel, watching as the other version of himself lowered his hand from his mouth, staring back from the meditation hall in Source.

The radio on Daniel's belt crackled and Raoul said, "Daniel, convoy is on the X. Pulling up in one minute."

He heard boots in the hallway behind him—members of the castle team heading to the front entrance.

He forced his attention away from himself in Source. He could suffer an existential crisis later. Right now, he had work to do.

Pat had been at the edge of the south woods just a few minutes ago. He couldn't drive back to the castle without being seen on camera, and there wasn't time to cross that distance on foot.

He didn't have to.

Create a painful situation, then offer an escape from the pain, Pat had said as they drove through the Spanish countryside. *They'll go where you want them to go, do what you want them to do, every damn time.*

Daniel sprinted for the hallway.

The castle's front doors stood wide open to greet the dignitaries, two security men stationed inside the doors. Raoul stood with Evan Sage and three others, just outside on the front steps. The convoy was already crossing the moat, almost to the circular drive, followed by the Range Rover from the front gate—the second follow-car.

Moondoggie behind the wheel. Pat's friend.

I'm gonna grab dinner with the boys, engage in a little pre-battle bonding.

Daniel kept running, almost there.

The follow-car stopped between the moat and the circular drive, as the rest of the convoy pulled into the drive and around. The convoy came to a stop one by one, drivers and bodyguards disembarking to open rear doors and hold umbrellas for the dignitaries.

Raoul started down the front steps, toward the president of Latvia, who was stepping out of his car.

"Raoul!"

Raoul stopped and turned and Daniel reached the front steps just in time to see Moondoggie toss a smoke grenade, creating a screen between the attack team and the rest of the convoy. A gunshot rang out, the round pinging off the castle's stone wall.

Security men grabbed dignitaries, shoving them down behind the cover of the SUVs, as two more smoke grenades sailed into the driveway. More gunfire from behind the smoke and Evan Sage pitched forward, clutching his gut, face first into the gravel.

Raoul started to rush forward. Daniel grabbed his arm.

"Raoul, your evacuation route is compromised."

And that's when Raoul Aharon's head exploded, showering Daniel with blood and gore. Raoul's body crumpled and rolled down the steps.

Daniel bolted back inside, the gunfight raging behind him. He ran the length of the main hallway at full speed, his heart pounding, but a part of his mind was calm now, focused on how Pat's plan would unfold.

Moondoggie's not attempting an assassination. No chance a half dozen mercs could win that battle—they were way outgunned—and Pat would know that. No, this attack was meant to trigger Raoul's evacuation protocol . . .

Visualizing the floor plan from the briefing file, Daniel turned and ran through the dining hall, down a short corridor, and through the kitchen to the castle's back door.

The security team out front will lay down covering fire, get the dignitaries into the castle, and follow this same route . . .

He ran into the rear yard. The gunfire continued out front, the attack team keeping everyone pinned down. Smart. *Make them work for it, just a bit, and they'll never suspect they're being led.*

Daniel kept his speed up, running past the line of waiting escape vehicles to the drawbridge, where he held down the button to lower it.

And the security team will drive the target straight into Pat's crosshairs . . .

There was nothing Daniel could say to stop them. His only chance was to get there first.

The drawbridge came to rest and Daniel hopped into the nearest SUV and cranked the motor to life. He threw it into gear, stepped on the gas, and tore off across the bridge and into the back meadow, heading for the south woods.

✦ ✦ ✦

Daniel turned the key and opened the door to Noah's rooftop palace. He thought of Kara for a moment. Whatever happened on the other side of this door, at least she knew how he felt. He took a deep breath and stepped through the doorway, into the light.

The light blinded him at first, but as his eyes adjusted, it settled to a cool blue-white. Still too bright—he had to squint—but not painful, and it didn't make him feel queasy anymore.

Maybe this was what glimmer looked like from the inside, or maybe something about Daniel had changed.

No, not from the inside. The glimmer was above him, a dome maybe twenty feet over the rooftop, and all around, stretching down to meet the edge of the roof. He was not *inside* the glimmer, but *beneath* it and *beside* it, *surrounded* by it.

Impossibly close, yet he felt fine.

Something about him had changed.

He raised his head and squinted straight up into the glimmer. He could see fractals in it. Moving, merging, growing, shrinking, evolving, appearing and disappearing, but never coming to rest.

It was beautiful.

It's just a swirling dance of energy and information. Digger's words on the beach came back to him full force, as if she were in his head again.

He lowered his eyes from the glim above, and Noah's rooftop palace revealed itself not as a palace at all, but just a rooftop.

Noah stood at the far edge of the roof, maybe forty feet away, right next to the glim. Daniel could barely make out his figure in the light, and he couldn't tell if Noah was looking at him, but he could feel Noah's strongest emotions. The confidence was unchanged, and with it Daniel could feel a sense of intense concentration . . . but not directed at him. Was it possible Noah still didn't know he was here?

Daniel crept forward, keeping his footfalls quiet as he closed the distance one agonizingly slow step at a time. Closer now, he could see Noah was facing away from him.

Facing the glimmer.

About twenty feet away, Daniel could make out more detail. Noah was doing something with his arms, gesturing with them just above his eyeline.

Daniel stopped about ten feet behind Noah, and his stomach fell. Noah's hands were almost touching the glimmer as he gestured, so close his hands and wrists shimmered, almost merging into fractals themselves.

And the glimmer itself was shifting in response to Noah's gestures. He was manipulating the very stuff of creation. As he worked, the fractals in front of him organized themselves into a cohesive image, like a photograph appearing in front of his eyes. An image of a crowded city street, but Noah flicked his wrist leftward and the image turned on an angle and slid to the side before Daniel could identify any details.

Then Noah made another image, and this one Daniel saw clearly. A long line of tanks rolling down a country road. Noah flicked it to the left and it came to rest parallel to the first image.

And then another: soldiers marching through an Eastern European city square.

Another: a massive peace protest turned violent, in London's Hyde Park, demonstrators fighting riot police.

—An American aircraft carrier battle group, moving at speed, white wakes streaming behind.

—A full meeting of the United Nations General Assembly.

—A political rally, but so much worse. Something right out of Leni Riefenstahl's *Triumph of the Will*, but not Nuremberg and not 1934.

It was Washington, DC, and soon to come.

Noah reached out and rearranged the photographs, putting the Hyde Park protest after the carrier battle-group deployment.

Tim Trinity and Angelica Ory and Kara and Daniel and probably hundreds of thousands of other people around the world with AIT had all been overcome by visions that later came true as real events on Earth. But Noah was not having visions, he was making them. Creating the future—the self-destruction of the human race—out of glimmer, with his own hands.

Daniel lunged forward.

Almost casually, Noah turned and reached his right hand straight to the side and then whipped it forward, pointing directly at Daniel, and a spike of blue fractals shot out from the glimmer wall and slammed into Daniel's chest.

✤ ✤ ✤

Daniel pressed the accelerator pedal down hard, keeping as much speed as he could on the wet gravel, barreling south toward the woods, now less than two thousand yards ahead and closing fast. The rain had settled into a steady shower, and the wiper blades on their highest setting could just keep up with it, swiping back and forth in front of his eyes, like the pocket watch of an overcaffeinated hypnotist.

He stole a glance in his rearview. The convoy of escape vehicles was well past the drawbridge, less than fifteen hundred yards behind him. They could see him from that distance—maybe if he radioed a warning, he could convince them he'd spotted a sniper ahead.

He grabbed for the radio on his belt, cutting his hand on something sharp. He glanced down. The radio had taken a bullet, the hard plastic shattered. He tossed the radio on the passenger seat.

Running out of options . . .

Driving straight ahead meant driving straight into Pat's crosshairs. There was a stand of evergreens ahead on the right. If Daniel could get behind the stand of trees and to the end of it, he could approach Pat on his left flank, using the trees for cover. But if he left the road and cut across the meadow too soon, he'd lose speed, and the convoy would close the distance and get to the woods before him.

He had to stay on the road and keep his speed up as long as possible.

He thought about the other Daniel—the one in the meditation hall in Source. Maybe that guy was having more luck. Maybe he could disrupt the meditation.

But so what if he did? Beating Noah wasn't enough. If Pat made this shot, war would follow. And millions would die, whether the ribbons touched today or next week or next month.

And then Daniel saw Pat's SUV ahead, parked in the middle of the gravel road, just inside the edge of the woods, facing this way.

Close enough to take the shot? Maybe. If not yet, then any second now.

Daniel held his breath and kept his speed up, almost expecting his chest to bloom red at any moment, as Tim Trinity's had on that outdoor stage in Jackson Square.

He shot a look at the stand of trees ahead on the right.

Just a little longer . . .

He glanced in his rearview again. The convoy was gaining, but still out of range.

Hold your nerve . . .

He reached across his body and did up his seatbelt.

Just a little longer . . . NOW.

Daniel swerved right, easing off the gas. He bounced wildly across the grassy meadow and two wheels came off the ground and he thought he might be going over but he steered into it in time and the wheels came crashing back to Earth and his jaw slammed shut, making him see stars.

He spat some blood and a piece of tooth onto the floorboards, straightened the wheel, and gave the car more gas, making it to the cover of the evergreens.

But the convoy had kept to the road and was now coming into range.

And just beyond the trees, less than twenty yards away, Daniel saw Pat, rifle in hand, now standing on the driver's seat of his SUV, torso rising through the sunroof, aiming straight down the road.

✦ ✦ ✦

The bolt of fractals retreated back into the glimmer wall, leaving Daniel flat on his back, convulsing on the rooftop, his electrical system misfiring. He'd never felt such agony. He struggled to raise his head. Noah stood over him, watching with what looked like mild curiosity.

"I suspected Pat wouldn't be able to kill you. He's a bit sentimental that way. But it doesn't really matter if you die there or here. You can die knowing that he's completing his mission at this very moment."

Daniel tried to get his body under control, tried to sit up, but he could do nothing but lie there, twitching. The glimmer behind Noah shifted and the images suspended there began to lose focus.

Noah turned back to them, leaving Daniel prone and helpless and sure he was dying, remembering the first night he was hit by AIT, back in Barbados. He'd dreamed of a bolt of lightning hitting him in the chest. The vision had recurred several times, and Daniel now understood it had been a premonition of this moment. His last moment.

Once Noah's attention returned to his task, the images became clear again, and he went straight back to work creating new ones.

—A city on fire at night.

—Thousands of dead soldiers strewn across a battlefield.

—A B-52 bomber, raining its payload down on Moscow.

—Radioactive snow falling on the ruins of Manhattan, covering it like a poison blanket.

—Nuclear blast shadows of civilians left on sidewalks and the walls of buildings.

Daniel could only watch as Noah created these horrors and organized them into a narrative of the future, setting up the dominos that would draw Earth closer until the ribbons touched and the dream ended.

He could feel the purity of Noah's intention. Not moral purity, but the powerful thrust of pure intention, untainted by doubt or any uncertainty. Noah continued to project confidence in his success, but that was all.

No anger, no hatred. This was simply the most efficient way to get what he wanted, to sweep away the universe containing Earth so he could create a new dream in his own image. He was utterly indifferent to the suffering he was causing but he didn't feel hatred, and that horrified Daniel even more than if he had.

The opposite of love is not hate, it's indifference. Tim Trinity had said that many times during Daniel's childhood, warning the boy to stay away from people who could turn their feelings off like flipping television channels.

If Daniel was going to die now, he didn't want to die bathed in Noah's indifference. He closed his eyes to the horrors unfolding in front of him, and he focused his mind on the opposite of indifference.

He thought of Kara and the intimacy they'd shared, and it hurt, but the pain was real and Daniel pulled it close to his chest. He thought of Tim, the deeply flawed father figure who had loved him and treated him with kindness, and who had warned him about indifference. And he remembered the gut-wrenching pain he'd felt cradling Tim in his arms as he died. And he thought of Pat, and the pain he'd felt when he learned what Pat had become.

But all this pain came from love, and as Daniel allowed it all in, he gained strength from it, and he used the strength of that pain to block out the physical pain, and he struggled to his feet and moved forward with lurching steps, picking up speed, rushing at Noah.

Noah felt it coming. He spun to face Daniel, his arm raised to draw down a new bolt of glimmer, but he was too late.

Daniel wrapped his arms around Noah, and together they plunged off the rooftop and into the glimmer.

The images Noah had created scattered through the spaceless space, growing dim and distant and then disappearing altogether, and Daniel thought he could feel the ribbons moving apart.

And then Daniel felt himself slip away, as he and Noah both dissolved into fractals.

40

D aniel skidded to a stop behind the trees. He grabbed the rifle from the back seat and checked that a round was chambered, opened his door, and hit the ground running for the last tree in the stand, desperate to get close enough to call out to his friend, to try one more time, to say something that might reach through the madness and make Pat see what he'd become, remember what he once was, to make Pat see something beautiful in life, to make him see that this was a dream worth saving.

But as he ran, his peripheral vision picked up the convoy, now within Pat's range.

Too late. He was out of time.

Daniel stopped and braced himself against the trunk of the last tree in the stand, fought to catch his breath.

Pat was fewer than ten yards away, lining up his sights on the approaching convoy.

"Pat!"

Daniel raised his rifle, sighting down on his best friend.

Pat turned his head from the scope and looked straight at Daniel, held his gaze for a moment, and Daniel thought maybe he'd reached him.

Then Pat swung his rifle, barrel sweeping toward Daniel.

Daniel squeezed the trigger, killing his best friend.

EPILOGUE

Bathsheba, Barbados

Daniel tied his tie again, thinking, *Third time's the charm.* But this time it came out too long. He undid the knot and started over. There was a knock at the door.

"Come in, if you know how to tie a tie."

The door opened and Julia Rothman bounded in.

"Hey, stranger!" Julia gave Daniel a hug and a kiss on the cheek. "Congratulations!"

Daniel said, "Thanks. Glad you could make it."

"Wouldn't be anywhere else, silly. *And* I know how to tie a tie." She reached forward and proved it.

"Thank you." He checked her handiwork in the mirror. "Couldn't have done it better myself."

"Obviously. Little nervous, are we?"

"Nervous in a good way," said Daniel, returning her smile.

"Big step."

"Nah," said Daniel, "the big step was a year ago. Just took a while to convince Maya to make it official."

It was a fun way to tell it, but it wasn't exactly true. Daniel thought back to the first night after he and Kara returned to Barbados, lying naked on tousled sheets in Daniel's little cottage, spent and happy, listening to the tree frogs outside. After a while, Kara had said, "It feels like quantum entanglement, baby. You and me, from now to forever, like we're permanently connected on some subatomic level." And that was that. They hadn't spent more than a day apart since. The real reason they'd waited a year was to be sure the Ian Shefras and Maya Seth identities hadn't been compromised, before making it legal.

Julia smirked. "Maya, huh? And I'm really supposed to call you Ian from now on?"

"Yep," said Daniel. "That's who I am now."

"Okay . . . *Ian*," she said, trying it on. "What about Pat, does he have a new name, too?"

A brief surge of grief washed over Daniel. He still missed his best friend, and despite everything, he wished Pat could be here to stand as his best man.

"Pat died a year ago. A hero's death, fighting to make a better world."

"I'm so sorry."

He deflected it. "Pat always said he'd never live to cash a Social Security check." Pivoting to a happier subject, "I almost forgot—your paperback's out next week, right? When do we get volume 2?"

"Be a while, I'm afraid," said Julia. "AIT didn't wane, didn't taper off—it just bloody well vanished. Like one day there's maybe a million people on the planet with AIT, the next day, zero. Like something shoved it out of existence. We haven't uncovered a single case since the day it went away."

"I know, I saw you on TV." Daniel had no idea what his other half had done in Source, or what had become of him. But on the day Daniel killed Pat, AIT had vanished again, leaving no trace behind. As it had so many times throughout history, Daniel supposed.

"Maybe it just got bored," said Daniel, "and decided to mess with someone else's universe."

Julia said, "My publisher keeps throwing money at me but they'd really like a book one of these days. Meanwhile there's no phenomenon to examine, so I'm living under a mountain of medical reports from those who were being studied while it was here, trying to glean anything worth publishing. It remains a mystery. And it may remain so until AIT returns, if it ever does."

If Julia someday managed to solve the mystery, she'd have another smash hit on her hands. But in the year since AIT vanished, the world kept turning and the public calmed as people got on with their lives, integrating whatever they thought AIT had been into whatever metaphysical world view felt comfortable. Fitting it into their *reality tunnel*, as Dana Cameron had once said.

The public never learned of the attempted assassination at Arlington Manor, the trade summit quietly shelved for later. The G7 session had gone ahead as originally planned, downscaling tensions by a notch, which as it turned out was enough.

And as the Earth rolled once again around the sun, humanity had narrowly missed several flashpoints, failing to trigger a new global war, settling back to the not quite global war that passed for status quo.

Risen apes, thought Daniel. *Risen apes lashing out at the darkness, treating each other with savagery and tenderness, stumbling one step forward, two back. Two steps forward, one back. Ever onward.*

Julia was saying, "And what about you? What's in store for Ian Shefras?"

Daniel crossed to the window and looked out on the Roundhouse's patio, one floor down. It had a perfect casual Caribbean charm, with white linen tablecloths and pink hibiscus everywhere, and John Holt playing on the stereo—and a stunning view of the Bathsheba hillside, down to the Atlantic Ocean, shimmering turquoise under a cloudless sky.

The small party mingled on the patio, sipping champagne. Like Julia, Ayo had flown in from New York, but the rest of the party was made up of local friends. Friends from their new life, who knew them only as Ian and Maya.

He said, "You know I never had a father, and after I left my uncle I spent my whole life seeking one . . . in Father Nick, in the Church, in God ultimately, or whatever I thought might be behind AIT."

He looked back out the window as Kara—Maya—stepped out onto the patio wearing the light-blue strapless dress they'd bought last week in Holetown. She was carrying their son on her hip.

Daniel said, "I'm done looking for fathers. Having too much fun being one."

"What's his name?"

"Tim."

"Perfect," said Julia. "He's beautiful."

"They are." Daniel waved at Kara from the window. She smiled and held the boy up and waved his little hand in response.

He pulled back from the window and checked himself in the mirror one last time, said to Julia, "How do I look? And feel free to lie."

"You look like a happy man," said Julia, "and that's no lie."

"See ya after."

As he got to the door, Julia said, "Raised by a preacher, spent a decade as a priest . . . it's funny, I know you left it behind, but I still would've figured you'd have gone for some sort of church setting."

Daniel said, "Look out the window. That is my church."

He walked down the old circular stairwell and through the restaurant, considering Julia's question.

What's in store for Ian Shefras?

He honestly didn't know. The time with AIT and the time he'd spent in Source felt almost like some dream he'd had. A dream that was now fading in memory, as dreams do. At the time, it had been so real that his life on Earth had begun to feel like a dream.

Daniel felt occasional pangs of grief for Source itself—for the loss of such an intensely sensate life, the freedom of spot-traveling, the intimacy of feeling another's emotional state almost as your own. But it didn't really matter. Earth contained all he needed.

And maybe Earth was a dream, but it was the only dream we've got. Daniel would go on dreaming it with the people he loved. He was done fighting against those trying to make it a bad one, becoming like them in the fight.

Ian Shefras would spend his life making it a better one instead.

He stepped out onto the sun-drenched patio and wrapped his arms around Maya and Tim. He took the boy from Maya and flew him around that patio, making airplane sounds as Tim burst into giggles.

"Okay, little man," he said. "You're gonna hang out with Uncle Natty, while Daddy gets married." He handed the giggling boy off to Natty B, then he took Maya's hand and walked with her to the edge of the patio, where they stood with the ocean behind them.

He looked into her green eyes. "Hey, you."

She winked at him. "You ready?"

"Couldn't be more ready," he said. "Girl of my dreams."

THANKS AND PRAISES

I might be the luckiest guy in the world. Not only because I get to play with my imaginary friends for a living, but because I do so with the support of such incredible people.

Dan Conaway: super-agent, friend, fellow lunatic. Also Simon Lipskar, Maja Nikolic, Taylor Templeton, and the whole gang at Writers House. And Lucy Stille, my film agent at APA.

The extraordinary publishing team at Thomas & Mercer: Gracie Doyle, Jacque Ben-Zekry, Alison Dasho, Caitlin Alexander, Sara Addicott, Lindsey Alexander, Karen Parkin, Tiffany Pokorny, Timoney Korbar, Mikyla Bruder, Jeff Belle, Sarah Shaw, Dan Byrne (great name!), Kjersti Egerdahl, Kim Bae, Christian Fuenfhausen . . . brilliant to work with, one and all.

Luke Daniels narrated the hell out of these books. I'm blown away by his performance, and couldn't be happier with the audiobooks of this trilogy. Much thanks to Luke, and to everyone at Brilliance and Audible.com.

I'm also lucky to have such amazing early readers and brainstormers, who also happen to be loved friends and family. Barbara Chercover, Marcus Sakey, Blake Crouch, Dan Conaway, Greg Seldon, and . . .

. . . the love of my life, Martine Holmsen (aka: Agent 99), who I get to wake up beside every morning.

Finally, to Firedog, with a love beyond the measure of words. This book is for you.

ABOUT THE AUTHOR

Sean Chercover is the author of the bestselling thrillers *The Trinity Game* and *The Devil's Game* and two award-winning novels featuring Chicago private investigator Ray Dudgeon: *Big City, Bad Blood* and *Trigger City*. After living in Chicago, New Orleans, and Columbia, South Carolina, Sean returned to his native Toronto, where he lives with his wife and son.

Sean's fiction has earned top mystery and thriller honors in the United States, Canada, and the United Kingdom. He has won the Anthony, Shamus, CWA Dagger, Dilys, and Crimespree Awards and has been short-listed for the Edgar, Barry, Macavity, Arthur Ellis, and ITW Thriller Awards.

You'll find him at www.chercover.com or @SeanChercover on Twitter.